Gold Rush Bride Hannah

By Linda Shenton Matchett

March 1829

Dahlonega, GA

Chapter One

Reverberations from the gunshot echoed among the hills surrounding Hannah Lauman's property as she gripped the rifle and watched the cougar disappear through the trees. Winter had apparently not been kind to the gaunt and shaggy animal, prompting its boldness to approach the homestead. Fortunately, Quinn had taught her to shoot, so she could protect herself during the times he was away from their claim. Four-legged beasts weren't the only predators she'd had to scare off after word got out about how much gold she and her husband were pulling from Yahoola Creek.

Despite a chilly gust that tugged at her skirt, perspiration trickled down her spine and pooled under arms. No matter how often she used a gun, she'd never get used to the thunderous boom or the weapon's kick against her shoulder. She'd sport a bruise by nightfall. She reloaded the rifle, then leaned the gun against the clothes-line post next to the basket filled with wet laundry. She needed to be ready if the big cat decided to return. Would she ever get used to living so remotely?

Hannah wiped the sweat off her forehead with her sleeve, then blew out a deep breath. Philosophizing over her lot in life wouldn't get the chores done, and she had plenty to complete before Quinn's return by dinner, provided he wasn't late. Some women had to worry about their husbands' penchants for drinking, gambling, and other detrimental pursuits, but Quinn's worst habit was getting caught up in the beauty of the outdoors and losing track of time.

Panning this week had been more productive than usual and storing the accumulated flakes and nuggets in the cabin was never a good idea, so today's journey to Gainesville was his third trip to the bank. How long the gold would hold out was anyone's guess, so she should probably be down at the water's edge, but the two of them were out of clean clothes, and she hadn't swept or dusted in days. She wasn't so gold-hungry that she'd live in a pigsty.

She grabbed one of Quinn's shirts and hung the cotton garment over the line, then bent and picked up another. She ought to warn the other miners about the wildcat, but perhaps the gunshot would bring one of the neighbors running so she wouldn't have to seek them out. She continued to hang the laundry, periodically glancing over her shoulder in case the cougar decided to return. Known for their humanlike screams, the tawny cats crept with silent stealth when on the prowl.

Finished with the clothes, she gave one last look toward the forest, then picked up the basket and headed toward the cabin. Inside, she lit one of the lamps to push away the gloom from the small abode. She'd put her foot down when Quinn suggested they build a soddy, but some days the tiny two-room abode didn't seem much better. With only one small window next to the door, the interior remained dim except on the sunniest of days.

"Hello, the house!" A shrill voice sounded in the yard.

Hannah stepped to the doorway and waved.

Glenda Thompson, the wife of another miner a few claims away waddled toward her, the woman's swollen stomach evidence of her late-term pregnancy. She carried a towel-wrapped bundle. "Good afternoon, Hannah. I made several loaves of bread and thought y'all might be able to use one."

"Real bread sounds heavenly. We've been eating biscuits with most of our meals. Quinn will be thrilled."

The petite blonde woman handed her the loaf, then rested her arms on her belly. "Where is that husband of yours? I didn't see him on my way over. Thought he'd be down at the water with the rest of the boys sifting through the sand."

"He went into Gainesville. Should be back any time."

"Another trip to the bank?" Glenda's eyebrow lifted. "Y'all must be doin' better than the rumors say."

Hannah shrugged. "Quinn's no Stephen Girard. We won't be financing the government any time soon."

Glenda giggled, then sighed. "At least you're gettin' by."

"Not quite the thrills and riches we were promised, huh?" Hannah tucked a stray hair behind her ear. "We've done better than some, but the work is backbreaking, and the worry about claim jumpers, injury, and wildlife is wearing." She snapped her fingers. "By the way, a cougar wandered into the yard a short time ago. You might have heard the gunshot."

"I thought Quinn might be huntin' squirrels or rabbits. That's bad news about the wildcat. I'll be sure to pass the word." Glenda huffed out a breath. "You ever wonder what life would be like if you weren't diggin' for gold day in and day out?"

"More often than you'd think." She gestured to the garments flapping on the line. "If you'd have been here earlier, you'd have heard me arguing with myself. Like I said, we're doing all right, but I miss the conveniences we had in Atlanta as well as the socializing. It gets lonely." Especially with no children, but Hannah wouldn't get into that. Married for nearly ten years, she'd yet to conceive. And the longer her childlessness went on, the farther apart she and Quinn grew. She shook her head to clear the morose thoughts. "Everything okay?"

"We've about played out our claim. Might be movin' on." Glenda's chin trembled. "There are a few claims available upriver, so Bart's thinkin' of buying one of those. This was going to be our chance to get ahead. Scrimpin' by on a blacksmith's income before comin' here was better than this. I'm not sure how much more gold chasin' I can do, but Bart doesn't listen to me. He's sure we're gonna strike it big."

"He might not be wrong. Quite a few claims have produced significantly." Hannah rocked on her heels. "We only found dribs and drabs when we first arrived. We kept at it, and finally hit a good vein."

"Yeah, but we're gonna have a family to think about soon. We need a stable salary." Glenda rubbed at the cross dangling from a long silver chain around her neck. "I've been prayin' Bart will come to his senses, but nothin' yet."

"I'm sorry things are hard for you." Hannah fiddled with the edge of the towel. If their claim hadn't produced, would Quinn have been willing to walk away? Go back to their staid life in the city? If truth be told, they'd done better working the gold. A bit of a dreamer, he'd held and lost numerous jobs over the course of their lives together, always moving on to opportunities that were supposed to be bigger and better. The day he'd come home and announced he'd purchased a gold claim from a widow, they'd argued well into the night. Then she'd decided that working together might sweeten their marriage, draw them close again. She was still waiting for that to happen. What was it with men and their desire for fortune and glory?

Thundering hooves pounded, and Hannah's head whipped toward the sound. Chet Fawley, Dahlonega's sheriff crouched low over his horse's neck. He brought the animal to a halt, then slid from the saddle. His face with lined with fatigue and sadness.

Hannah's stomach hollowed, and her hand flew to her throat. There was no doubt the man brought bad news. "Quinn?" Her lips moved, but no sound came out.

Sheriff Fawley removed his dusty Stetson and licked his lips. "I'm sorry, Miz Lauman. Your husband's dead. Ambushed outside of town."

Dizziness struck, and she swayed. Glenda wrapped her arm around Hannah's shoulder, keeping her from falling to the ground in a heap. Dots of light danced in her vision, and roaring, like an approaching train, filled her ears. A lump formed in her throat. "Ambushed?" Her voice caught, and she swallowed. "Who would want to murder my husband?"

"Looks like the work of the Cherokees. I've got my boys looking into things as we speak." He ducked his head. "I guess you'll be pulling out and going back to Atlanta, so be sure to let me know how I can contact you when I solve the case. Shouldn't be long."

Overhead, the sun broke out from behind a bank of clouds casting a bright beam onto Hannah's face. A slight breeze brushed her cheeks as if God had reached down to remind her of His love and presence, even during this terrible turn of events. Hannah squared her shoulders. "I'm not going anywhere, Sheriff. I've got a claim to work."

March 1829

Knoxville, TN

Chapter Two

The midday sun heated Jess Vogel's back as he hunched over the makeshift table to repair the wheel from the farm's largest wagon. Sweat trickled down the sides of his face, but after the long, frigid winter, he relished the unseasonably hot day. There would be plenty more cold temperatures, and perhaps snow, before plowing could begin in April.

His stomach rumbled, and he tossed the hammer on the table. He pulled out his handkerchief, removed his broad-brimmed hat, and wiped the moisture from his face. Stuffing the cloth back into his pocket, he wandered into the barn and grabbed the pail of food he'd prepared before leaving the house. He dropped onto a small hay bale and reached into the bucket for one of the thick ham sandwiches.

Salty flavor exploded in his mouth as he took a bite of the succulent meal. Chewing slowly, he surveyed the interior of the building. Still lots of tasks to be done before his boss's farm would be ready to welcome the change in seasons.

He began to estimate how many days he had left to get things done, and the muscles in his neck tightened as he realized the date. The food in his mouth turned to sawdust. He swallowed, then tossed the sandwich into the bucket. How could he have forgotten? Today was supposed to be his wedding day, but thanks to the scarlet fever that swept through their small community six months ago, he was performing repairs on his prospective father-in-law's farm instead.

Memories bombarded him. Picnicking by the creek with Arabella. Watching the moon rise from the front porch. Sitting in her parents' parlor reading aloud from their favorite book, Walter Scott's *Chronicles of the Canongate.* He frowned. Scott's book was the last thing they read together as she lay in bed, fever raging. When Nathaniel let him keep Arabella company in her bedroom, he should have realized her parents held no hope for her recovery.

Sweet Arabella. They'd known each other since birth, their properties abutting in the Pennsylvania countryside. Without siblings, the two were drawn together from a young age, exploring the woods and fields, sharing chores, and walking side by side to school, until her parents decided she'd had enough education. She'd blossomed from a gangly, awkward youngster into a lithe and graceful young woman, so when her father approached him to arrange their marriage, he'd been agreeable.

But then President Madison declared war on Britain, and as part of the state militia that was federalized, Jess had been called to serve. And life was never the same since.

"Jess." Nathaniel trotted toward him, waving an envelope. Arabella's death had grayed her father's hair and etched additional lines on his face, but even at nearly sixty-five, the man was still strong as an ox. "This arrived by post from Georgia."

Jess heaved a deep breath and forced a smile. He took the letter and glanced at the return address: Dahlonega, Georgia. Who did he know in Georgia? His forehead wrinkled, and he stuffed the missive into his pocket.

"Aren't you going to open it?" Nathaniel tilted his head. "Could be important."

"I've—"

"Listen, you don't need to hide things from me. I know you're miserable here. You need to make a fresh start. Go to a place where you're not plagued by memories. Somewhere you can be your own man."

"I'm not miserable."

"Pretty close to it, I'd say." A sad smile curved Nathaniel's lips. "You're a good man, Jess, and your willingness to wed Arabella after she rejected you for another all those years ago is commendable. But she's gone, and there's no reason for you to stay."

"Agreeing to marry her was the right thing to do. Too many years passed before she got over that ne'er-do-well. I was happy for the opportunity to provide her with some happiness."

"And now it's your turn. You deserve joy, and you're not going to find it toiling on my farm. If that letter is a response to an inquiry you've made, you should read it. We'll miss you, but we'll be fine should you choose to leave."

Jess pulled out the letter. "But that's just it. I didn't write anyone, and I have no friends in Georgia."

"That you're aware of." Nathaniel's eyes twinkled.

"That I'm aware of."

"All the more reason to open it."

"If you insist." Jess retrieved the envelope and broke the wax seal. As he scanned the scrawled words, his eyes widened. He raised his gaze to Nathaniel's. "You've got your wish. I'm headed to Georgia."

"Looks like you've seen a ghost."

"I have. This is from Quinn Lauman. We met during the war and hit it off immediately. More than once we saved each other's life. Before we mustered out, we promised that if one of us ever had a serious need, we'd contact the other." He waved the parchment. "Quinn's in trouble."

"How so?" Nathaniel pursed his lips.

"Listen...

Dear Jess, I'll bet you're surprised to hear from me after all these years, but I'm in danger, and I knew exactly who to contact for help. I live in Dahlonega, Georgia now, having arrived a few months ago after hearing reports of gold. I've been somewhat successful and got a nest egg built up at one of the banks. But there have been a bunch of incidents over the last few weeks that make me fear for my life and my wife's. That's right, Jess. I managed to find a woman who loves me. And I've got to protect her. Please come as soon as possible and help me find who's trying to run me off my claim.

Your friend, Quinn Lauman

Crossing his arms, Nathaniel sent Jess a piercing look. "You don't know what you're walking into. You could get hurt...or worse."

"Yes, but a promise is a promise, and he wouldn't have asked if he wasn't desperate." Jess tugged at his shirt collar. "I'm sorry to leave you in the lurch, Nathaniel, but I've got to head out first thing in the morning. It's been over two weeks since this was sent."

Nathaniel nodded, then clapped him on the shoulder. "Absolutely. I'll tell Prudence so she can pack some food for you."

Jess studied the straggly script on the page, and his pulse quickened. Perhaps he could make his fresh start in Georgia after he helped Quinn. As long as he didn't get killed in the process.

Chapter Three

The last notes of "Amazing Grace" hung in the air as Pastor Woods intoned the benediction. Hannah bit back a sob as the miners and their wives shuffled forward to toss handfuls of dirt on Quinn's plain wooden coffin. A burst of wind tugged at the pins in her hair, and she pulled her coat closer to her body. After the last of the mourners headed to the cabin where Glenda had set up a table for the food, Hannah bent and gathered a fistful of Georgia red clay. She extended her hand over the cavernous hole that held her husband and let the soil filter through her fingers. Clumps thudded on the casket. So final a sound.

"Come to the house, Hannah. The boys will finish up here." Sheriff Fawley put his hand to the small of her back, then gestured to the crowd that milled around the yard. "You don't need to stay and watch."

Their faces filled with pity, two of his deputies leaned on their shovels a short distance away.

Another gust blew through the clearing, bringing the pungent scent of pine trees. And something else...the aroma of new growth. The irony was not lost on her. She sucked in a deep breath and nodded. Time to move toward the future. A future without Quinn.

She allowed the sheriff to lead her toward the table, where he filled a plate for her from the variety of dishes her neighbors had brought, as if food would somehow dull the sharp pain of loss and regret. She and Quinn would never have a chance to reconcile. She smiled her thanks and listened with half an ear to people who murmured condolences and well-meaning advice.

When she and the sheriff were finally alone, Hannah narrowed her eyes at him. "Have you had any success finding the Indians who did this? Quinn deserves justice, and I want to see someone punished."

"We're doing the best we can, but clues are scarce. There were no witnesses, and the braves we talked to were less than forthcoming, most claiming ignorance of English. Besides, they're not going to implicate one of their own."

"Excuses." She hurled the plate onto the table where it landed with a thump. "We shouldn't have to live in fear. Why are the Indians still here? This is our land. They don't belong."

"Those are harsh words, Hannah." He shrugged. "The government is doing what it can, but the situation is tenuous, and you don't want to hear this, but the Natives were here first."

"We bought this property fair and square, all of us."

"Yes, but things aren't so cut and dried with regard to the Indians. My deputies and I are working to solve Quinn's murder, but you have to give us time. Don't rile things up."

Hannah shoved her fists into the pockets of her skirt. "I don't think it's too much to ask for you to find my husband's killer. That can't possibly be *riling* things up."

He pushed his Stetson back on his head. "Look, you're upset. We've just buried Quinn. This conversation is for another day. Now, I've asked Bart to give you a hand with packing your things so you don't have to do it alone."

Hannah's gaze whipped to the sheriff's face. "Thanks, but I don't need any help. Quinn didn't have much. Just his clothes, shaving stuff, and..." Her voice caught, and she swallowed. "I can handle the few items."

"I meant packing up the house." He tilted his head. "There's nothing for you here. Aren't you going to sell and move back to Atlanta?"

"So if I can't be a wife, I'm of no use?"

His face flamed. "No. I mean, you could look for a job, but there's not much to be had in a town this size."

"The lack of support for women on their own is appalling. If gals can't marry some guy or teach his children, they're stuck working the saloons, or worse, the brothels." She pulled herself to her full height. "Why can't society let us do more than that? It's ridiculous."

"Well—"

"I'm staying, Sheriff. Our claim is still good, and I see no reason to run home with my tail tucked between my legs."

"You can't be serious."

"Why not?"

"Why not?" His color deepened as he sputtered. "Because it's a dangerous place. For men, but especially for a woman alone. I can't let you do it."

"Excuse me?" Hands on her hips, she glared at him. Who did he think he was telling her what she could or couldn't do? "What law prevents me from working the claim on my own?"

"None, but Quinn's death should be proof that it's not safe for you to stay. My boys and I can't watch you twenty-four hours a day."

"I'm not asking you to."

Sheriff Fawley ducked his head. "There is another option...you could marry me."

Hannah gaped at him. "Marry you? I've just buried my husband, and you're asking for my hand?"

"It's not like that. Forget I asked. You're looking to stay. I was trying to help."

She winced. "I'm sorry, Chet. That was rude of me. You're a good man, and I appreciate your offer. But I'm going to do this on my own—"

The sound of an approaching horse cut through her words. She turned and studied the lone rider on a magnificent ebony stallion. Wearing a black cowboy hat pushed high on his forehead, he sat tall in the saddle.

A six-shooter was strapped to his lean hips, and long, tapered fingers had a firm grasp on the reins. The horse was one of the largest she'd ever seen, well over seventeen hands if she guessed correctly.

Beside her, Sheriff Fawley stiffened and moved his hand over his gun. "Are you lost, son?"

"I don't think so. This is the Lauman claim, right?"

Hannah's stomach hollowed. Who was this man?

"Yes." Sheriff Fawley puffed out his chest. "But I don't see how that's any business of yours."

She laid her hand on his arm. "I can handle this." She stepped forward. "I'm Hannah Lauman. What's your interest in my land?"

The man slid from the saddle, reached into his vest pocket, and held out a folded piece of paper. "I'm Jess Vogel, and I got a letter from Quinn asking for my help." His voice was as smooth as warm honey.

A harsh laugh escaped as she took the paper from his hand. "You're too late. We just buried him, not thirty minutes ago." She had to give this Jess his due. His eyes widened only slightly, and he maintained his composure.

"Then it's even more imperative that I stay."

Great. Another man thinking she needed to be protected.

Jess yanked his hat from his head. "I'm sorry for your loss, ma'am. Quinn and I go way back. To the war. We were in the same unit."

She seemed to study him, her beautiful face filled with skepticism. "He never mentioned you. Do you have any proof?"

His gaze bounced from her to the bearlike sheriff next to her. One false move or statement, and they might be burying him if the lawman was as good with a weapon as he seemed. Jess clutched the brim of his Stetson. "Just the letter, ma'am. I mean you no harm."

The paper crinkled as she unfolded the missive. Her lips moved silently as she perused the words, then she stroked the parchment with a trembling finger. Her face ashen, she returned the letter. "Okay, so you knew my husband. What do you want?"

"To be of service. Whether it's working the claim with you or helping find who did this to Quinn makes no nevermind to me."

"The last thing I need is some man elbowing his way in on my claim."

"You misunderstand." He spoke as he might to a colt he was trying to break, pitching his voice low and steady. "I don't want any of the gold. I owe Quinn my life, so I'm in his debt. He's gone, so the debt transfers to you. I'll do whatever you need, but I'm not leaving."

The sheriff glowered at him but remained silent.

"What if I don't want you to stay?" Her eyes glittered, sparks of hurt mingled with anger and uncertainty.

He put on his hat. She was a pistol, no doubt about it. "Then I'll look for your husband's killer."

"Good luck with that. All the evidence points to the Cherokees, but they're not talking, and no one saw anything."

Jess shook his head. "The Indians aren't interested in your gold, but there must be plenty of white men who are. Quinn mentioned some incidents in the letter, but didn't include details. Would you be willing to tell me about them?"

Uncertainty flitted across her face, and she glanced at the sheriff, then back at him. He pinned on what he hoped was an encouraging expression. He'd go behind her back if he had to in order to keep her safe and find Quinn's killer, but secrecy was fraught with pitfalls.

"Have you eaten?" Resignation and something akin to hope warred for supremacy in her eyes. She gestured to the house. "I'm sure there are plenty of leftovers."

"That's mighty kind of you. I left before sunup this morning. A meal would be appreciated. Would you mind if I unsaddled Major?"

"Not at all. We've got oats in the barn. Help yourself."

"Thanks. Much obliged." He dipped his head and led the horse into the ramshackle structure. He couldn't hear the sheriff's words, but from the man's tone of voice, he wasn't happy at Mrs. Lauman's decision to feed him. Would she let him stay?

He made quick work of removing Major's tack, then brushed him down and fed him. He stroked the animal's muzzle. "Good boy. Not much of a stable, but it will have to do until I can make improvements. Wandering out of the hut, he looked for a pump so he could wash up, but didn't see one. Did she have to haul water from the creek? His estimation of the woman grew.

The yard was vacant, and he smiled. She'd managed to get the sheriff off her property. Bet that had taken some doing. Jess strode across the uneven expanse and onto the tiny porch. He rapped his knuckles on the doorframe.

"Come in."

He stepped inside, and the aroma of frying chicken greeted him. His mouth watered, and his stomach rumbled. Standing in front of the stove, Mrs. Lauman had donned a white apron over her dark blue dress. Despite the fatigue that lined her porcelain complexion, she was exquisite. A golden-brown braid hung down her back, and her eyes were the color of a summer sky.

Blinking, he shook his head. What was he doing admiring his friend's widow mere hours after his burial? He cleared his throat. "I didn't expect you to cook for me." A plate piled with biscuits waited on the table next to a glass of water. The tiny cabin was scantily furnished and dim. Couldn't Quinn have provided a real home for his wife?

"I'm just reheating some things. It won't be long." Her gaze raked his attire. "There's a pail of water in the sink for washing."

Aware of his perspiration and travel-weary clothes, he nodded. "Guess I should have stopped in town, but I didn't want to waste another minute. The closer Major and I got, the more pressure I felt to get here." He slipped past her, the clean scent of her hair wafting toward him.

Lavender? He swallowed and dunked his hands in the pail, then used the lump of soap to scrub his hands and face. By the time he toweled off, she'd set the food on the table and was sitting in one of the two rustic chairs.

Dropping into the vacant seat, he bowed his head. *Lord, You've got Your reasons for allowing Quinn to be killed, but I can't imagine what they are. Comfort Mrs. Lauman, and help me know what to do. Thank You for her kindness in feeding me…and for not throwing me out on my ear. Amen.*

He looked up and grabbed a couple of biscuits.

"You're a believer?" Her voice was hard as steel.

"Yes. You?" He took a bite of the flaky bread.

"At one point, but I'm not exactly on speaking terms with God right now."

"Understandable." He continued to eat. "You're hurting awfully bad."

She gaped at him. "You're not going to tell me I need to rest in His comfort. That he has a plan in all this?"

"Nope. I figure plenty of people have already done that." He wiped his mouth on the cloth napkin. "Don't get me wrong. I agree with them. God is the only One who can stop the pain, but you already know that. No sense in telling you stuff you already know, but I will be praying for you." He pulled out the letter and laid it on the table. "Quinn asked for my help. Please let me stay. I promise you won't regret it."

Would he?

Chapter Four

Hannah swung her feet onto the floor, the cold boards shooting chills up her legs. Her eyes gritty from the long and sleepless night, she climbed from the bed. Shivering, she hurried to the dresser, lit the lamp, then poured water from the pitcher into the basin to wash up. She dressed in the dim room and pinned her hair into a bun at the base of her head before straightening the covers on the bed. A bed she'd never share with Quinn again.

Her gaze fell to his clothes hanging on the hooks. A lump formed in her throat, and she buried her face in the shirts, breathing deeply of his scent. Tears formed, and she let them fall. Giving in to her sobs, she cried for several minutes, her wails filling the room.

Drained, she squared her shoulders and wiped the moisture from her cheeks. If she were on speaking terms with God, she'd tell Him what she thought of His plans for taking Quinn. But prayer was a waste of time, so she returned to the bureau, dipped a cloth in the bowl, and washed her salty skin.

With a loud sigh, she scrutinized her red, blotchy reflection in the mirror. Crying hadn't done her any good, and now she looked haggard. Hopefully, by the time she gathered the eggs, fed the animals, and finished breakfast, her complexion would return to normal. She needed to get down to the river and couldn't let other miners see any sort of weakness.

At some point, Sheriff Fawley would probably show up and make another attempt at convincing her to sell her claim. She gritted her teeth and marched out of the bedroom to prepare her food. She was not going to let anyone run her off. She might have been reluctant to come when Quinn had pitched the idea, but such as it was, this was her home. Until the claim quit producing, she'd work the vein and save her money.

After a quick meal of scrambled eggs and leftover biscuits, she slapped together a couple of sandwiches and wrapped them in a towel. She grabbed the last few cookies and put everything in a pail. She rinsed her dishes and left them in the sink. Enough time had been wasted. She needed to get to the river.

Lunch in hand, she opened the door and gasped. Quinn's friend, Jess, stood in the yard, arms crossed and looking just as handsome as he had yesterday. Her heart thundered in her chest. He'd promised to return this morning, but she hadn't believed he would. What sort of man takes on the problems of a friend he hasn't seen in a decade and a half? "Mr. Vogel."

He bowed and removed his hat. The rising sun glinted off his ash-blond hair. His chocolate-brown eyes were unreadable. "Mrs. Lauman, you seemed surprised to see me. I made a vow and intend to keep it."

She studied him for a moment and seeing no guile, she shrugged. "Suit yourself. I was just heading down to the claim. You're welcome to join me. Supplies are in the barn."

"That's what you're wearing?" His forehead wrinkled, and a frown twisted his mouth.

And so it began, a man with no authority over her criticizing her choices. Her stomach clenched. She glanced down at the denim pants and flannel shirt that clad her body, then stomped a booted foot. "If you had ever tried to pan for gold in a dress, you'd understand my outfit. I can't slog through the water in skirts. Now, you can either accept my way of operating and give me a hand, or you can hop back on your horse and head back where you came from."

Holding up his hands as if in surrender, he said, "Forgive me. I've seen a lot of things in my time, but never a woman dressed like you, so your attire is somewhat of a shock."

"Many of the women who pan wear pants. You'll have to get used to it."

He plunked his Stetson back on his head. "I'll do my best, but first we need to discuss the situation before more time passes."

"Daylight is burning. I've got chores to do, so you'll need to talk while we work." She set the pail on the ground and strode to the barn, Jess close to her heels. She swallowed a grin. If he was this easy to boss around, maybe having him here would be a help after all. They entered the shack, and she gestured to the pony. "If you feed and saddle him, I'll take care of the chickens and gather the eggs. Then we'll grab our tools and get out of here."

As she scattered the corn, the chickens clucked and pecked at the kernels. Behind her, Jess scooped oats into the trough, then gathered the tack. He was an efficient worker, she'd give him that. She snatched the eggs and put them in a basket, pleased at the number. Maybe she could make a cake later, giving her something to do during the lonely evening.

She wandered to the corner of the shack where the mining tools were stored and hissed in a breath. The implements were gone, every last one of them. A shiver slithered up her spine. The items had been in place last night. She'd seen them while feeding the pony. While she'd tossed and turned, someone had crept in under cover of darkness and filched them. Heat flushed her body, and she fisted her hands. "How dare you steal my livelihood!"

At her shout, the pony snorted, and the chickens scattered.

Jess rushed to her side. "I'm not."

"Not you." She pointed to the empty corner, the urge to cry or kick something warring within her. "I've been robbed. That's where the mining tools are supposed to be, and they're gone."

"I stayed in town last night against my better judgment, and this is proof that it's too dangerous for you to be here alone. We should find a place in town for you to live, and we can come out each morning to work the claim."

"No. If they steal from me while I'm here, what sort of damage will they do if I'm absent. And I think there's some law that says if I vacate the property, I could lose it. Not going to let that happen."

"All right, then I need to bunk here, but I'm concerned for your reputation."

"I've little care for what others think of me. You can stay in the barn. I'll provide linens and a pillow, so you're not totally bedding with the animals. And if we're to be working together, let's dispense with formalities. Please call me Hannah."

"Sounds perfect." Grinning, he held out his hand. "I promise to work hard and not get in the way."

Hannah grasped his warm, calloused fingers, tingles shooting from her palm to her elbow. Loathe to admit it, she was glad to have the help, but why did he have to be so good looking?

Chapter Five

Pulling Major to a stop, Jess slid from the horse and gaped at the crowd of men crouched at the creek's edge. Like ants at a picnic, the number of miners was countless and just as silent. Nearly identical in attire and stance, each man hunched over the water, hat worn low on his head, squinting into a pan. No one looked at them or spoke, and the only noise was the scraping of shovels against rock.

He glanced at Hannah, who stood next to the pony unpacking her saddlebags. They'd lost the entire morning going into town to replace her tools and report the robbery to the sheriff. The man had made a valiant effort to convince her of the danger of remaining in the boomtown and working her claim, but his words had fallen on deaf ears. The longer he talked, the stiffer Hannah's posture became. By the end of the conversation, her jaw and hands were clenched, but she was gracious when she assured him of her plans to stay.

They'd returned to the cabin, eaten the lunch she'd packed hours earlier, then headed to the creek as the sun hit its zenith in the cloudless blue sky. Perspiration had already formed at his hairline and trickled down his back. He'd be soaked by dinnertime.

Tying off Major under the trees, he grabbed his supplies and followed her to the water. Squatting next to her, he mimicked her actions. "You'll have to give me a primer on what to do. This is my first experience searching for gold. What makes this place so good?"

She gestured to the rushing water. "The floods from winter storms and the spring snowmelt wash fresh gold down from the mountains. Another couple of months and the water level will drop, and panning will get more difficult. Eventually by midsummer, the creek is dry, so folks will find somewhere else to pan or get a job. I've heard lots of reports about who found the first gold, but the stories differ wildly, so it's tough to know who to believe."

"How'd you and Quinn hear about it?"

Her shoulders stiffened, and he regretted bringing up the memory.

"It was about this time last year. We were living outside of Macon." Her eyes took on a distant stare. "The fall harvest had been poor, and we were struggling to make our payments. Quinn took some odd jobs here and there, but being winter, work was scarce. He was looking for a way to make money, and some of the men in town were talking about it at a church social. That night he told me he'd sold the farm. Within three days we were here." Her lips thinned. "We had enough money to pay off what we owed and build the cabin."

"You mentioned that Quinn was killed coming home from making a bank deposit. You're doing all right with the claim?"

"Yes, better than we could have imagined."

Jerking his head toward the swarm of men, he narrowed his eyes. "There seems to be plenty to go around. Why did he think he was in danger?"

"We had a few incidents like the tools, but he never intimated we were in serious trouble." She shuddered, her face pale. "The sheriff wouldn't let me see him and said the Cherokees were responsible for his death, so he must have been scalped."

"What motive did the Indians have?"

"This is mostly their land, but after the gold was found, the government started working to get them relocated. The Indians knew it was here. That's why they named the area Dahlonega. The word means yellow money in their language."

"But why Quinn? If they don't want the miners here, why not attack with a war party and be done with it?"

"That's my train of thought, and why I'm not convinced the Cherokees killed him." She gripped the pan. "And why I'm going to stay and work the claim. I'm not going to let some bully run me off. If I leave, whoever killed him will have won."

She drew herself to her full height, and he swallowed a grin. A hairsbreadth over five feet tall, she looked ready to take on the world regardless of her diminutive size.

"And we can't let that happen. So, tell me what to do with this armload of tools."

Her face pinked. "I'm ranting again, aren't I?"

"I admire your spirit."

Hannah pointed to the shovel. "First, you're going to scoop a few handfuls of gravel, sand, and silt out of the creek into the pan. Be sure everything is nice and wet. The gold is heavier than the other stuff in the river, so if you shake the pan and swirl the water, the gold will settle at the bottom. Then tip the pan into the water and let the current carry away the silt and sand. You've got to be careful not to let too much of the material get away. Repeat the process until you've got a small amount of the sand. As you continue to swirl the pan, the flakes will settle further, and you pick them out."

"You make it sound simple."

"Simple, yes. Easy, no. Every muscle in your back will be screaming by the time you're done." She put on a pair of leather gloves. "Your hands may not need covering, but the first time I panned I got blisters so bad I could barely move my fingers. They'll save you from cuts and scrapes, too. Eventually, you're going to need to dig in the cracks and crevasses of the rocks, and some of them can be sharp."

Jess sat back on his heels. "Don't you sound like an old hand."

Her color deepened, and she ducked her head. "I've learned a few things over the months."

He nudged her shoulder. "Don't be embarrassed. You're a smart gal. I'm impressed with your knowledge."

She shrugged. "No smarter than anyone else."

"I beg to differ, but enough conversation. I'm going to find you some gold." He snatched up one of the shovels and a pan, then bent over the water. His first attempts at imitating her gentle motions were an abysmal failure. He was too heavy-handed, his movements abrupt and awkward, dumping the sand back into the creek in clumps.

Tongue peeking out from between her lips, and her brow furrowed in concentration, Hannah worked quickly and efficiently. He huffed out a sigh. At the rate he was going, he'd be lucky to collect half an ounce by day's end. At least he could rest in the knowledge he was keeping her safe. For now.

Time passed, and he finally got the hang of the process. Huddled on a large rock in the middle of the swollen river, she dipped and agitated her pan. She worked for several minutes, then rose and pressed her hand against her lower back. "I could use a break." She hopped from one boulder to the next. As she landed on the one closest to shore, her ankle twisted and her foot plunged into the deluge. Losing her balance, she fell face-first.

Jess leapt to his feet and lifted her from the water. She weighed little more than a child. He laid her on the ground, then wiped the wet strands of hair from her face. His heart banged against his ribs. So much for keeping her safe. "Are you all right?"

Eyes screwed shut, and she moaned. "My ankle. I wrenched my ankle."

He looked up, but none of the miners appeared to notice her accident. Apparently, it was every man for himself. He frowned and shook his head. "This may hurt a bit, but I'm going to remove your boot. We need to see how bad the damage is."

Her lips in a thin slash, she nodded.

With delicate motions, he untied the laces on her boot, loosened the gusset, then slid out her foot and rolled down her sock. She sucked in a breath. His gaze shot to her face. "I'm sorry. There's no discoloration or swelling, but you should probably check in with a doctor."

She sat up, her face wan. "I guess we're done for the day. A stupid move on my part. I should have been more careful. Can you help me get things loaded?" She grimaced. "And I'm going to need help getting on the horse."

"You wait right here." He gathered the tools and shoved them into the saddlebags, then returned to where she reclined. "Nice day for sunbathing. Sure you don't want to stay for a bit?"

"Ha ha. I'm more than ready to leave." She attempted to stand, but winced and fell back to the ground.

"Easy now." Jess swept her into his arms, and she laid her head on his shoulder, with a sigh. The fragrance of her soap assailed his nose, and the feel of her slight form against his chest sent his heart pounding. He gave himself a mental slap. The poor woman was only days from being widowed. He had no right to be affected by her closeness. Too bad his skittering pulse didn't agree.

Chapter Six

The pain in her ankle had subsided to a dull throb, but Hannah was grateful for Jess's help dismounting the horse and getting settled on the rickety-looking rocking chair inside the cabin. He arranged the quilt over her lap, then went to the stove and started the coffeepot. Moments later, the acrid aroma of the dark brew wafted toward her. She laid her head back and closed her eyes with a sigh. Between the theft and her stupidity at falling, the day had been almost a complete waste.

As soon as Sheriff Fawley heard about her accident, he'd start haranguing her about leaving again. What did Jess think about the mishap? With the exception of asking how she felt a couple of times, he'd been stoic during the ride back from the claim. When she'd trained him how to collect the gold flakes, he'd seemed impressed, but had she doused his admiration with her clumsiness? Would he pity her? Praise himself for being here so he could rescue her?

Hannah rubbed her forehead. Too many questions and not enough answers. China clinked, then footsteps clomped toward her. She opened her eyes as he approached bearing a cup, his forehead creased with concern. She forced a smile and held out her hands to take the coffee. "Thank you." Her face warmed. "And thank you for helping me with...you know..." She gestured to her legs.

"No need to thank me. It's what friends do." He crossed his arms. "Would you like me to ride into town for the doc? You should have the ankle checked."

"No. I'll be fine by tomorrow morning, perhaps tonight." She took a sip of the dark brew. "Mmm. Where'd you learn to make such good coffee? I think this just became your job."

"Changing the subject, are you? I'll play along." He folded his lanky frame into the nearby chair. "My mother taught me her secrets, but I'll never tell."

"Hello, the house!" The sheriff's voice sounded from the yard.

Jess rose, opened the door, and gestured for the lawman to come inside.

Sheriff Fawley yanked off his hat and strode to the couch. "Some of the boys down at the river told me you hurt your leg. Is it serious? You should have seen the doctor." He tossed a glare over his shoulder at Jess, then knelt by her side. "I could ride for the doc or send for him."

Hannah set down the cup and squeezed his arm. Why did every man think she needed saving? "I'm fine. Or I will be. It's just a twinge. That's all. I didn't watch what I was doing and turned my ankle, but the joint isn't swollen, and the pain has subsided for the most part. I'm going to keep off it for the day."

"You need to be more careful, Hannah. I told—"

"Stop. I appreciate your concern, but please don't lecture me. I was foolish and paid the price, but the accident wasn't serious. Jess helped me, but any of the guys could have if he wasn't here, so save your criticism, and tell me why you came all the way out here."

"Fair enough." His mouth twisted, looking like he'd eaten something bad. Rising, he crossed his arms. "I wanted to let you know I haven't had any luck finding the Indians who killed Quinn. I know the chief within the local tribe, and he never ordered any attacks, and none of the braves have bragged about killing a white man."

"And you believe him? He might be protecting his own."

"Could be, but I doubt it. I've known this guy for a while, and he's straight up." He plunked on his Stetson. "Anyway, I wanted to let you know I'll keep looking, but the trail cools every day that passes."

Her stomach roiled, and she pressed her hands against her middle under the quilt. "So I shouldn't hold out any hope? Quinn deserves justice."

Jess stepped forward. "He's doing his best, Hannah. Solving a murder takes time, but you do have to prepare yourself in case we can't find the culprit. Dahlonega's a big place, easy to get lost in." He reached into his pocket and withdrew Quinn's letter, then handed it to the sheriff. "Quinn seems to think someone wanted his claim. That kind of motive doesn't sound like an Indian. You had any complaints about claim jumpers? Maybe the killer staged the murder to frame the Natives. Wouldn't be the first time that sort of thing has been done."

The sheriff tapped the letter. "You might be right. If Quinn suspected the Indians, he'd have said."

"What can you tell us about the claim, Hannah?" Jess tilted his head. "Did Quinn get one during the original lottery, or did he purchase from someone?"

The rolling in her stomach turned into a knot, and Hannah set her jaw. How much should she tell him? A chill swept over her. Now that he knew the value, perhaps he saw an opportunity to get rich. Did he want to determine if he could take the claim from her? Her gaze bounced from his face to the sheriff's. Who could she trust?

Disappointment, anger, fear, and suspicion danced across Hannah's cheeks, but Jess refused to break eye contact with her while she studied his face. She didn't trust him. Did she think he was out for her money? Should he tell her he had plenty of his own and that he didn't need hers, or would that admission make matters worse?

She blew out a deep sigh and rubbed the back of her neck. "Quinn didn't share his business dealings with me, but he did tell me he bought the claim from a woman whose husband had died. Her name was Sadie Webb. He came down here one day without telling me and took care of the transaction. After he secured the property, he came back to Macon and told me to pack."

Jess's eyes widened. No wonder Hannah got testy when she felt he'd been dictatorial. The sheriff, too. Quinn had apparently treated her as an ignorant and naïve girl. Hadn't he realized how smart she was or was he threatened by her intelligence? She might have helped him get a better deal if he'd included her. It was obvious she was pulling more than her fair share.

Sheriff Fawley returned the letter to Jess. "Where did Quinn store his copy of the deed, Hannah?"

"It's not here." She frowned. "Or at least I haven't found it."

"Okay. Maybe it was on him when he died, and the killer got it. I'll go to the gold office. But I'm not sure what that information will tell us."

"Can you also find out who applied for a claim but didn't get one?"

"Possibly, but that's not a likely motive. There are still plenty of sites to go around."

Jess frowned. "Yes, but what if our guy wanted a particular claim?"

"Could be. I'll see what I can unearth." Sheriff Fawley smiled at Hannah. "Care to go with me? Sweet-talking the clerk might go further than the heavy hand of the law."

The guy's actions made it obvious how he felt about the widow. Jess's stomach clenched. Surely she didn't reciprocate his feelings mere days after Quinn's death. Had the man been interested before his friend's demise? Was he an opportunist or worse? No. Jess was grasping at straws. Nothing in the man's behavior lent credence to him killing Quinn to marry his wife.

But that didn't mean she wouldn't eventually fall for the lawman.

Hannah shook her head. "That's not my style, Sheriff. The clerk would see right through me. No, I think it's best if you go without me, but I appreciate the offer."

A spark of irritation glinted from the sheriff's eyes for a split second, and Jess swallowed a grin. Not that he wished the man ill, but the last thing Hannah needed was the complication of a relationship. She needed time to mourn the loss of Quinn.

Jess schooled his features. "Guess it's too late in the day to make it to the office before they close."

Fawley shot him a dark look. "Yes, as a matter of fact it is, but the information isn't going anywhere, so first thing in the morning should be fine."

Pressing his lips together against a retort, Jess shoved his hands into his pockets. This from the man who'd warned them about the trail cooling as time passed. Did he want to solve Quinn's murder, or was he just making a show of it? Was a little digging about the lawman in order?

He glanced at Hannah's slumped shoulders and wan face. She was putting on a brave front, but the day had taken its toll on her. "Listen, we appreciate you coming by with the news, Sheriff, but Hannah could use some rest. I'll do some more hunting for the deed and any other documentation that might be useful for your investigation. We haven't checked the barn."

With a frown, the sheriff gave a curt nod, then wagged his finger at Hannah. "I'm available should you need me for anything." He jerked his head toward Jess. "Anything at all."

"Thank you, Chet, but I'm sure we'll be fine." Her chin trembled. "We'll hold down the fort here so you can focus on the case."

The sheriff gave him another long look, then yanked open the door and stalked outside. The door closed with a muted thud.

"I don't think your marshal likes me." Jess shrugged. "Not that I'm looking for new friends, but I hope that doesn't impede his ability to do the job."

"He's a professional, but for some reason he does think he needs to be my protector." Her mouth twisted in a wry smile. "Frankly, not much different than you've been acting since your arrival. You two may have more in common that you want to admit."

His face heated, and he sputtered, "We—"

"I'm quite worn out, Jess. I'm going to lie down. You're welcome to search the living area or the barn." She shoved aside the quilt and staggered to her feet, wincing as her right heel hit the floor."

He rushed to her side, swooped her into his arms, and carried her into the bedroom. He laid her on the mattress, then returned to the couch and grabbed the patchwork comforter to cover her. "Rest. I'll rustle up dinner." Before she could reply, he ducked out of the room and closed the door.

Grabbing his hat, he strode from the house. He needed to put distance between him and the attractive widow of his friend lying on the bed. Hopefully, the exertion of searching the barn would get her off his mind. He scrubbed at his face with cold fingers. Not likely, but he could give it a try.

Chapter Seven

Rain thrummed against the window like a snare drum, and intermittent thunder rumbled. A periodic lightning flash illuminated the greased paper pane. The storm had been raging since the middle of the night and showed no signs of abating. The lamp flickered, and Hannah tossed aside the book. She'd read *The Last of the Mohicans* too many times to care what happened to the Munro sisters, but the novel was one of only six books in the tiny cabin.

She rose from the couch and prowled the room, a slight twinge gripping her ankle as she walked. Her fall had been avoidable if she'd been paying attention. It wasn't the slick surface of the rock that had caused her to slip, but rather the vision of Quinn's friend hunched over the water on the bank of the creek. The sunlight hitting his silver-blond hair, and his long, tapered fingers working the pan. The final distraction has been the sight of his muscles straining against the fabric of his shirt.

"Get ahold of yourself, Hannah. You've been widowed less than a week. What are you doing cogitating over your husband's friend, who will be leaving at some point." She blew out a loud breath. "There are plenty of chores to be done. Get busy."

Marching to the kitchen area of the tiny house, she grabbed a broom and began to sweep with a vengeance. She finished the floor and attacked the ceilings, stabbing at the cobwebs that had formed. A housekeeper she was not. One of the few *wifely* tasks she was good at was baking. Her bread was light and flavorful, her desserts delectable. If she did say so herself.

"That's what I'll do. Baking always makes me feel better." She swept the dust into a pile, then brushed the debris toward the front of the house. As she opened the door to send the rubble outside, she startled.

Jess stood on the threshold, hand poised as if to knock. Eyes wide, he leapt back.

Hand pressed against her banging heart, she widened the door so he could come in out of the rain. She blinked as his scent wafted into her nose as he slipped past her.

He grinned. "You're so bored you've been reduced to cleaning the house. I'm glad I decided to see if you wanted company."

"You don't think much of my housekeeping skills?" She frowned and swept the pile out the door with a swift motion, then turned and held out the broom. "You could offer to do your share."

"That's not it. My mother hated to clean house and claimed most women felt the same. I figured you don't care for it either." He held up a small box, painted on both sides in a checkerboard pattern. "Care for a game or three?"

Her anger dissipated like dust on a windy day. "Yes. I love to play checkers. That's a lovely container. Where did you buy it?"

"I made it."

Hannah leaned closer and inspected the container. She'd been mistaken. The pattern wasn't painted on the box, but constructed of pieces of wood veneer glued together. Some sort of oil or varnish gave the box a satiny sheen. The decorative hinges and clasp were brass. "Truly beautiful. You've got a gift for woodworking."

"A hobby I picked up from my grandfather." When he spoke, his breath ruffled her hair.

She straightened and rushed to put away the broom, hopefully giving her pulse time to return to normal. What had she been thinking to get so close? She should have waited to admire the piece after they began to play.

After hanging the broom on the hook, she smoothed her skirts and frowned. She must look a fright. Would he think her vain if she went into the bedroom to check her appearance in the mirror? Bah. There was no reason to care how she looked. He was here to lend a hand, nothing more.

The chair thumped as he seated himself and set up the game. She sat across from him, then picked up one of the checkers. A perfectly formed disk with a tiny flag carved into the surface.

He turned the board so the black checkers were in front of her. "Ladies, first."

With a fluid motion, she made her move. "You were right, you know."

"How's that?" Jess looked up and smiled, his eyes crinkling at the edges. "I like to know when I'm right."

She giggled. "When you said I was bored. Like your mom, I despise cleaning the house. It's such a useless task. You clean away the dust and dirt, yet they return within hours. At least washing clothes or the dishes serves a purpose."

"Mom used to say the very same thing." He tilted his head. "The two of you would be fast friends."

Warmth spread through Hannah's chest. Why did it please her to know his mother would like her?

For several minutes, they played, silence enveloping the room, then he slid a piece forward and cleared his throat. "I was surprised to see the house was stick-built, not a soddy."

"I was...uh...pretty adamant about that. I promised to make Quinn miserable if he made me live in a mud hut." She lowered her gaze. "Not very nice of me, and he was right to be angry, but in the end he agreed that the cabin was a better place to live. Being able to come back to a house, no matter how small, was nice after a long day working the claim." She shrugged. "It's not perfect, but it's home."

"I'd be happy to make it perfect. As you can see, I'm not without skills. Up until now, I've done little to earn my keep."

Tears prickled the backs of Hannah's eyes. She nodded and shoved a checker forward, stalling until she could talk past the lump that had formed in her throat. Every time she'd asked Quinn to make a repair, he groused that he worked hard enough during the day and couldn't be expected to fix every little imperfection. Once, he'd told her to take care of the renovations herself if she didn't like how he'd built the place.

The last few weeks of his life had been filled with a series of arguments. She couldn't seem to please him in any way. After ten years of marriage, did all couples have difficulties? She pressed her lips together. Or was it just their relationship?

Rain continued to buffet the cabin, and Jess went to the fireplace to add more logs. The wood caught quickly, and flames burned brightly, casting an orange glow on Hannah's face. Her hair sparkled in the light, but her eyes were dull. She seemed grateful for his offer, yet troubled to do things around the house. The conversation had probably reopened the wound of widowhood. Hopefully, she realized he meant well rather than harm.

The fire crackled in the silence, and the flickering lamp on the table created a cocoon of light around them. He glanced around the room while she considered her next move, her fingers absentmindedly tapping a staccato rhythm on the wooden surface. Rather than feeling small and cramped, the house had a cozy atmosphere. The patchwork quilt draped over the couch was a rainbow of color. Quilted throw pillows were propped in every seat ensuring comfort. The curtains were simple drapes of gauzy white fabric of some kind, lending an airiness to the space. Wall hangings were few but also colorful and seemingly hung with an eye toward bringing beauty into the house.

As if the place needed any. Hannah's appearance outshone any of the material goods. Since the war, he'd been content with his singleness, focused on making a living and seeing no need to add a wife or family to the equation. Comfortable with his own company, he had no need for a large circle of friends.

He peeked at Hannah, who still stared at the checkerboard. A lock of hair had fallen free from her bun, and his fingers ached to rub the glossy tresses to see if they were as soft as they looked. A few days with his friend's widow, and he could easily see himself wed.

She slid her piece across the board, then sat back and put her hands in her lap.

"Are you letting me win?" He hopped two of her checkers. "King me."

Her face flushed. "No, but apparently my mind isn't on the game."

"It's been a tough few days, Hannah. Give yourself some grace."

"Yes, but I don't have the luxury of taking my time. I must continue working the claim, so I can make the payments."

"Surely taking a day or two to grieve is acceptable."

"Yes, but they'll think me weak."

"Who?"

"Whoever killed Quinn. I can't let them see me flinch."

He put his hand over hers to stop the tapping. She looked up, sadness and vulnerability etched on her face. His heart clenched. What burdens did this poor woman bear? "Well, whether you want the break or not, the weather is forcing itself upon us for at least today. And if it would make you feel better to talk about Quinn, I'm a good listener."

"I'm not sure what I can say. You knew him from the war. I doubt he's changed."

"Tell me about when you two met." Did he want to hear about this woman falling in love with someone else?

One shoulder lifted in a delicate shrug. "He showed up looking for work. Quinn is...was...a smooth talker, and my father hired him on the spot. To be honest, I don't know a lot about his history." She grimaced. "Foolish, I know. Anyway, from stories he told sometimes I discovered he spent the years after the war traveling around the country, picking up jobs wherever he could find them. He'd wrangled cattle in Texas, drove a stagecoach in Tennessee, and even worked as a sailor for several years, crossing the ocean many times. The war was terrible, so maybe he was trying to forget, but he seemed to become bored easily, always looking for new challenges." Her face darkened.

He wondered at the memory that caused her to frown. "How long did he work for your dad before courting you?"

"A few months, and we married a year later. At first, things were wonderful. We were in love and had a place of our own. Dad had carved off a small parcel and given it to us as a wedding gift. The farm did okay, but Quinn hated the long hours. You work sunup to sundown, and then some. But we kept at it. Time passed, and we kept hoping for a child." Tears trickled down her cheeks. "But months passed, then years, and we didn't conceive. We began to blame each other. I hoped things would improve after we moved here..." She swiped at the moisture on her face. "I'm sorry. It's not proper to have this sort of conversation."

"You're fine." He made an exaggerated show of scanning the room. "I don't see any of our high society friends. I think we're safe."

A giggle escaped, then she sobered up. "Thank you for being so understanding. And for your kindness."

"Always." He'd do whatever he could to assuage her grief and see a smile light her face.

Chapter Eight

Pink fingers of dawn seeped through the boards of the barn as Jess rolled over and stretched. The storm had blown over sometime after midnight, and the day held the promise of sunshine. He finger-combed his hair. Before falling asleep, he'd decided to build a rocking chair to replace the dilapidated one in the cabin, but before that he'd surprise her by making breakfast. The longer he could keep her off the injured ankle, the better she'd heal.

He climbed to his feet and changed into fresh clothes. Poking his feet into his boots, he made quick work of feeding the animals and collecting the eggs. He'd seen some potatoes in the pantry, so he'd rustle up some home fries. His biscuits were typically dry, so he'd skip those.

With a grin, he grabbed the pail of eggs, then hurried toward the cabin and tiptoed inside. He lit the stove and set the cast-iron skillet on the burner, then pared and cubed the spuds. Rummaging in the vegetable bin, he found an onion. Perfect. He diced the bulb and added it to the potatoes.

He realized he was humming and shook his head. Since when was he so domestic?

After dumping the potato and onion mixture into the pan, he set the table, then snapped his fingers. Coffee. His head was in the clouds. He went back to the stove and prepared the dark brew. With the potatoes nearly done, he scrambled four of the eggs and poured them in another skillet. The tantalizing aromas set his mouth to watering, and he glanced toward the bedroom. Glass clinked from inside, then a puddle of light shone from under the door.

His stomach buzzed as if a flock of starlings had taken flight. Trying to ignore the sensation as well as the thoughts of Hannah preparing for the day, he turned his attention to the stove. He wouldn't impress her if he burned the meal. A few more stirs, and the food was ready.

The door opened, and she shuffled into the living room wearing her regular attire of dungarees, flannel shirt, and boots. How did she manage to look so lovely in that getup? Crescent-shaped shadows hung below her eyes. The last few days were taking their toll.

He poured a large mug of coffee and set it on the table, then gestured for her to sit down. "M'lady, your breakfast is ready."

She gaped at him and remained in place, so he went to her and looped his arm with hers. "You don't want it to get cold."

Her chin trembled. "No one has ever made breakfast for me. It smells delicious."

Jess clamped his lips together to prevent responding. Granted, he'd only known her for a short time, but he couldn't understand Quinn's treatment of his wife. Alternately critical and neglectful, he failed to cherish the woman. What was wrong with the man?

After seating her, Jess dished their food and put her plate in front of her. He poured his coffee, then grabbed his plate and sat. "I'd like to say the blessing, if you don't mind."

Hannah nodded and tucked her hands in her lap.

"Dear Father God, we thank You for another day. We appreciate yesterday's rain which was good for the farmers' crops and giving Hannah a chance to heal. Could You keep us safe today? Thank You for providing the food we're about to eat. We ask these things in the name of Your Son. Amen."

"Amen." Hannah's murmur was barely discernable.

Was her heart softening toward God? Jess poked several potato chunks into his mouth. "How'd you sleep?"

"Better than expected. I don't want to admit it, but my ankle ached and woke me periodically." She ate some of the eggs and sighed. "These are divine."

"Probably not." He chuckled. "Food always tastes better when someone else prepares it, but thanks. It's not exactly haute cuisine."

She flushed, and they ate in silence. A few minutes later she set down her fork and pushed away the plate. "I'm sorry I couldn't finish."

"No need to apologize. I'm sure the pain has put you off your food a bit." He ate the last of his food, then took a swig of tepid coffee. "I need to go to town for supplies to make the repairs and whatnot. Care to join me?"

Her eyes lit, and she bolted upright. "Oh yes. How soon do you want to leave?"

He chuckled. "Apparently right away."

The pink on her cheeks deepened, and she giggled. "I did sound rather desperate, didn't I?"

"Understandable. The change of scenery is just what the doctor ordered. I can be ready in fifteen minutes. Is that soon enough?"

"More than enough." She jumped up from the chair and rushed into the bedroom. Moments later she returned.

Hands deep in the soapy water, Jess turned at the sound of her footsteps. Now it was his turn to gape. She was beautiful. She'd exchanged her gold-digging outfit for a long-sleeved, gray dress that hugged her in all the right places. Black, laced-up boots peeked from under her skirt.

Uncertainty clung to her features. "I don't have a black dress. Should I even be going out so soon after...well, you know."

Jess dried his hands and went to her side. "Yes, you should go. I'm not versed on all of society's dictates, but it's no one's business how you respond to your loss. Getting out will do you good. The gray is perfect, and you look lovely. You'll show up every woman in town."

She tugged at her collar, then wrung her hands. "Not likely, but it's nice of you to say."

Did Quinn never compliment her? With a deep sigh, he gestured to a basket by the door. "We still have plenty of leftovers, so I packed lunch. We can have a picnic." Rather than eat in a restaurant under prying eyes, but he wouldn't mention that.

"You've thought of everything."

His chest lightened as they made their way from the house to the barn and climbed into the wagon. Within minutes, they were trundling down the road toward town, the *clip-clop* of the horse's hooves muffled on the dirt surface. "Are there any stores you'd like to visit besides the mercantile?"

"Not particularly, but window shopping might be nice. I don't need anything, but sometimes it's fun to browse."

Letting the horse have its head, he loosened his grip on the reins. "Nothing at all? I thought all women loved to shop. My sister and mother can make a full day of it."

She shrugged. "I've learned to make do without. Besides, where would I put anything? You've seen the size of the cabin."

"Point taken."

The wagon rolled over a bump, and she fell against him, her hand grabbing his thigh. She pulled back as if scalded, and her face flamed.

"Excuse me—"

"Sorry—" Tingles shot up his leg and radiated to his chest. "Guess I better pay better attention to the road. Don't want to pitch you over the side."

Hannah snorted a laugh, then covered her mouth for a moment. Her eyes danced. "Perhaps you should install straps to belt us in."

"Not a bad idea. I'll get right on that."

"See that you do."

"Funny." He sobered up. "Meanwhile, God kept us safe as we asked at breakfast."

She tilted her head. "Do you really think it was Him?"

"I don't know, but I choose to believe so."

"That's the rub, isn't it? We have to make an intentional decision to believe. Faith doesn't come easily."

"Not for me." He steered the horse around another dip in the road. "But I'm okay with that. I mean trusting in God is like having a relationship with anyone. We have to make an effort to take part."

Her shoulders slumped. "But what about when He disappoints you? How do you feel then?"

"Sometimes hurt, sometimes angry, but I tell Him."

"You do?" Her jaw dropped. "Isn't that disrespectful?"

"He wants our honesty, Hannah, and He's big enough to take it."

Her gaze took on a distant stare.

Jess cast a glance skyward. *Dear God, I don't know what happened to make her fall out of love with You, but help me show her the way back. Don't let me mess this up.*

Chapter Nine

With her sleeve, Hannah wiped the perspiration trickling down the sides of her face. The early April sun felt more like the dog days of August. She glanced at Jess, who worked a few paces away, his shirt darkened with sweat stains under his arms and along his spine, accentuating the curve of his back. Her face warmed, and the heat had nothing to do with the weather.

She ducked her head and continued to pan. Scoop, swirl, tip, swirl, pick. Repeat. In the week since the trip into town, they'd settled into a routine. She'd awaken to the smell of coffee percolating, and he'd make breakfast while she packed their lunch. After eating, she'd wash the dishes and he'd dry them. They'd take care of the animals together, then come to the river. Sharing the load meant she could arrive at the claim earlier, and they could get a few hours in before the sun began to scorch the earth.

But sharing the load also gave her company. Jess was a good conversationalist, and his quick wit brought a regular smile to her lips. She didn't understand how, but there had been days when she was inches away from Quinn, yet her heart ached with loneliness.

"Here's a good one." Jess scooted toward her.

She flinched. Good thing he wasn't a mind reader.

"Hold out your hand." He wore a boyish grin that lit his face as if a beacon shone on his skin.

"What'd you find?" She extended her arm.

He dropped a nugget into her palm. "Nice, huh? I can see how easy is is to catch gold fever. You slog through the water for days on end to cull flakes, and then bam, you dig up a chunk that's worth as much as a month's worth of work. And suddenly you're willing to pan until dark."

"It is addicting for some."

"Not you?" He cocked his head. "Your pulse isn't racing with the thrill of finding this?"

Hannah shrugged. "No. The gold is a means to an end. There are things I want to do, and they all require money, so the more I can find, the better, but I'm not looking to get rich for the sake of being wealthy."

"Not even a little?"

"Not even a little." She rubbed the clump, then returned it so he could put it with the rest of his day's collection. "Sounds like you wouldn't mind being loaded."

He flushed, and she giggled. "A desire to be financially comfortable is nothing to be ashamed of." She gestured to the men scattered along the riverbank. "The hope of prosperity is why most of them are clawing at the ground. Hence, the nickname: prospector."

"What would you do if you became a woman of means?"

"First, I'd buy a piece of land nestled near the woods and build a home big enough to raise a family. Then I'd fill one of the rooms with as many books as it would hold and invite anyone who couldn't afford to buy their own to visit. They could borrow as many as they desired."

"A library?"

"A *free* library, not a subscription athenaeum. Mine would be for the masses."

His look held pride and admiration. "Well, aren't you something? Wanting to get rich to buy books for others."

Hannah froze. "There's—" The hair on the back of her neck prickled, and she glanced up. A dark-skinned brave stood at the edge of the trees. Her gaze shot to the rifle propped on their pile of goods six yards away.

"What?"

"An Indian." She spoke without moving her lips. "On the far side of the river. He's staring at us."

Jess turned and studied the young man dressed in leather pants, his bare chest glistening in the sun. Jess beckoned.

"What are you doing?"

"Finding out why he obviously wants to talk with us." He patted her hand. "He's alone and not dressed as if for war. You've got nothing to fear."

With fluid grace, the young man picked his way across the water, ignoring stares and glares from the other miners.

Climbing to his feet, Jess dipped his head. "Jess Vogel, but you probably already know that."

"Yes, and this is Mrs. Lauman." The brave touched his fingers to his forehead. "My name is Wohali. It is nice to meet you, ma'am. I'm sorry for your recent loss."

She gaped at him.

He smiled. "You're surprised at my ability to speak English."

"Better than many people I know."

"One of your missionaries came to my people many years ago to teach us about your God. He taught us your language, and we taught him ours."

"You didn't kill him?" She clapped her hand over her mouth.

"My chief felt his presence was mutually beneficial, and he wasn't intent on making us as white men. He respected our culture and our ways. Father Sean was a great man."

"Was?"

"He died when I was a child."

Jess cleared his throat. "You have something to tell us?"

"None of the Ani-Yunwiya, those you call Cherokee, killed your husband, Mrs. Lauman. He was murdered by one of your own, a man who felt betrayed."

Her heart banged in her chest, and dots of light formed in her vision. She couldn't faint. Not now. She rubbed her eyes. "Who? Do you have a name?"

"No, but I will continue to seek the information you desire."

She scrambled to her feet and held out her hand. "Thank you for coming. For telling me this."

Wohali's eyebrow lifted. "You believe me."

"I do. I'm not sure why, but I do." For the first time since hearing of Quinn's death, she had hope. Beside her, Jess stirred, and her smile fell. After the murder was solved, Jess would leave. Then where would she be?

Jess narrowed his eyes. The young man took a great risk coming to the river. Too many of the miners were hostile toward the Indians. He was glad Hannah had been polite and accepting.

Wohali shook Hannah's hand, then bowed at Jess. "If I find out more information that may be of help, I'll return. Again, my condolences."

"Thank you for coming forward." Jess tucked his thumbs into his belt. "Would you be willing to keep an eye on the claim and Mrs. Lauman? I would do the same for you and your kinsmen."

"I'd heard you were a fair man, not like many of the other white men." He glanced at the prospectors. "Now, I see the rumors are true. I can watch." He turned on his heel, forded the river, and disappeared into the trees.

Hannah rubbed her forehead. "Why do you think he came? I wasn't lying when I said I believed him, but I don't understand why he would bother seeking me out."

"Perhaps he hopes you'll have some sway with Sheriff Fawley. Wohali doesn't want his people blamed for a crime they didn't commit, and I doubt the lawman would take the brave's word. Just a hunch."

"I don't know about my convincing Chet. He's a decent man, but he's generally sure he's right."

"And you're the little lady?"

"Unfortunately, yes, but I will speak with him. He needs to consider all possibilities, not the most obvious or easiest."

"The Indians have suffered at the hands of the white men. Forcing them off their land is the least of our sins toward these noble people. They have every right to be angry and try to stop us."

"There is plenty of land to go around, isn't there?" Hannah squinted at him. "I've heard they're not interested in the gold, so why not give us this land and go somewhere else?"

Jess's chest tightened. How could she be so cold and calculating? "This has been their home for millennia. Isn't that worth something? Just because they don't want the gold, doesn't mean they should have to leave."

Her mouth twisted into a frown. "Do you think it's wrong for me to be here? Working the claim?"

"No. Quinn purchased this fair and square. Giving up your claim won't help the Cherokees or any other group of Natives."

Hannah looked toward the trees. "Do you think Wohali told us everything he knows?"

"What reason would he have for withholding information?"

She nibbled her lower lip. "He doesn't. I guess I'm used to the men I know using knowledge as power."

"I don't believe that's the case here." He gestured to the water. "Ready to get back to it, or would you like to quit for the day?"

"Too much daylight left. We need to keep working." With a last glance at the forest, she knelt by the water's edge and began to pan.

Her rigid shoulders told Jess the conversation with Wohali had upset her. Whether it was the interaction with the brave itself or the report he brought, Jess didn't know, but she was definitely unsettled. Should he try to soothe her with words or leave her to her thoughts?

He snatched his pan from the ground and crouched a short distance from her. He needed to maintain his space. All Quinn had asked him to do was figure out who was causing trouble and protect Hannah.

But the assignment didn't include falling for the woman. She'd indicated her marriage to Quinn's hadn't been the best, but they must have loved each other, and she'd be grieving for the near future. He'd do everything in his power to find Quinn's killer, keep her safe, and help her work her claim. Nothing could come of their friendship, but he'd do his best by her.

Then he'd hightail it out of Dahlonega. Find somewhere to settle where he could forget the beautiful widow with the sparkling blue eyes and hair the color of cinnamon.

Chapter Ten

Huddled under a blanket on the couch, Hannah sneezed into her linen handkerchief. A perfectly good day for panning, yet she was laid low with a spring cold after managing to stay well throughout the entire winter. She sniffled and closed her eyes. Her limbs were heavy, and her throat scratchy. She'd been exhausted after trudging back to the cabin from the outhouse. Working the claim was out of the question despite the gorgeous weather.

She glanced at the clock over the mantel. Jess wouldn't be back from the trip into town to pick up supplies for another hour, maybe more. He'd offered to keep her company, but she insisted it made no sense for both of them to be useless. The lack of his presence lent an air of emptiness to the room. How had she grown to depend on him in a mere three weeks' time?

Quinn stared at her from the wedding portrait her parents had given them as a gift. A playful glint in his eyes and the slight curve of his lips made her wonder what he'd been thinking about while the artist painted them. She tended toward practicality and seriousness, but he was an eternal optimist, playful and impish which had been fun in the early days of their marriage. As time passed, she yearned for him to take the lead in their relationship. When he finally had, she found herself in the Georgia mountains panning for gold.

Was it time to pack up and return home? Why was it so important to stay and prove she was capable of working the claim? Her fellow miners certainly didn't care. In fact, they probably wished she'd sell off. More than a few had reminded her prospecting was no job for a woman. Sheriff Fawley had intimated the same thing. She balled her fists. Why did men think they were more capable than women?

Jess's image floated into her mind. Not all men felt that way. Not once since his arrival had he suggested she sell or stop working the claim. Instead, he made repairs around the property, helped with chores, and panned for hours on end without asking for anything in return.

What was his story? Handsome, intelligent, and kind, he must be nearly thirty years old. Why had he never married? Or had he lost a wife? He'd not mentioned one, and he didn't wear the aura of grief, but that didn't mean he wasn't widowed. Dare she ask him?

If she'd sold as soon as Quinn had died, she'd be at her parents' home nestled in her girlhood bedroom. Reclining on a fluffy mattress with a down comforter pulled up to her chin. Mother would prepare all her favorite dishes, and Father would read to her. She wouldn't have to lift a finger, rested and refreshed rather than worn out from trying to prove herself. But if she'd left, she wouldn't have met Jess.

She rubbed the back of her neck, then threw the blanket aside and swung her feet onto the floor. A deep sigh escaped. Granny would tell her that activity was the best medicine for the doldrums. Jess had washed the dishes and picked up the clutter, but she could look for Quinn's deed. The document hadn't been returned with his body, so it had to be somewhere in the house.

Starting in the kitchen, she removed everything from the cabinets, then ran her fingers along the back wall searching for a hidden compartment. Quinn had told her about a friend whose family found a secret cubbyhole filled with cash and jewelry after the father or grandfather had died. At the time, Quinn and she had laughed about the fact they owned nothing worth concealing. He'd been responsible for building the house. Had he included a cubby of their own?

Hannah finished exploring the kitchen and returned the dishes to the cabinets. Her head pounded from the exertion, and she leaned on the counter trying to catch her breath. She surveyed the small cabin, and her gaze fell on the door to the root cellar. A perfect place for safekeeping. She grabbed a towel and wiped the perspiration from her face, then picked up the lantern. Inside the cellar, she waited for her eyes to adjust to the dimness. The earthy smell of potatoes, rutabagas, onions, carrots, and turnips mingled with the pungent odor of dirt.

Holding the lamp at eye level as she inspected the walls of the small enclosure, she periodically pressed the wood with her fingers in an effort to make it pop open. Sweat formed along her hairline and on her upper lip as she worked from one end of the room to the other. Nothing. Her shoulders slumped, and a lump formed in her throat.

"Where did you put the deed, Quinn?" She swallowed a sob. "And what got you killed?"

If she had been a better wife, maybe he would have been more forthcoming with her. He'd accused her of being a nag whenever she questioned him, saying he'd tell her anything she needed to know. Which he'd never done.

Footsteps sounded overhead. Jess was home. Her pulse quickened, and she swiped at her eyes. She forced a smile and ascended the stairs into the house, then stopped short at the sight of Asa Bennett's hulking form rummaging through the stack of books near the couch.

"Asa, how dare you march in here and go through my things."

"I knocked." He dropped the book with a thud and stuffed his hands into his pockets.

"And I didn't answer, which means you shouldn't have come in." She set down the lantern and crossed her arms. "You need to leave. Right. Now."

With a smirk, he looked down his nose at her. "You and what army?"

A chill swept over her. He could break her like a twig. Her gaze went to the shotgun over the mantel. She'd never reach it before he got to her. "What do you want?"

"I'm here to get what's rightfully mine."

"Which is?" Fear morphed into irritation. Would the man never get to the point?

"The claim."

"What makes you think it belongs to you? Quinn purchased it fair and square."

Asa's face darkened. "It was mine first, then he swept in and snatched it up."

"You're saying he stole it from you? What proof do you have?"

"What proof do *you* have that you own this place?"

"Look, if you think Quinn did you wrong, take me to court. Meanwhile, get out of my house." Her voice trembled, and she pressed her lips together.

He lumbered toward her. "You think you're better than the rest of the miners. Wearing men's clothes and working the claim like a man. But you're just a woman, and accidents happen. Mining is dangerous. You could get hurt real easily, and nobody'd think much of it. You—"

Like a rag doll, he was jerked away.

"You shouldn't pick on people who aren't your size, mister." Jess held the man by his collar and the back of his pants. "Now, it seems to me the lady asked you to leave. If you go quietly, I won't drag your sorry self to the sheriff and press charges."

Hannah nearly wept in relief.

Asa clawed at his throat where his shirt pressed against his neck. "We...was...just...talkin'."

"That's not the way I see it. This is a limited time offer that expires in thirty seconds. I suggest you take it."

"Okay...okay."

Jess shoved him toward the door, and he stumbled, then caught the doorframe.

He pointed his beefy finger at the two of them. "You haven't seen the last of me." He yanked open the door and stomped outside, slamming the door behind himself.

Hannah ran to Jess and threw herself in his arms, pressing herself against his chest. His heartbeat was slow and steady against her ear. "Thank you. Who knows what would have happened if you hadn't returned."

With circular motions, he stroked her back, sending warm tingles up her spine.

"I may be wrong, but intimidation seemed more his style than actual violence."

"Well, it worked." She shivered.

"You're safe now. From here on out, you're not to be alone. Understood?"

She nodded and nestled closer to him. He'd get no argument from her. In fact, she'd stay like this as long as he let her.

Chapter Eleven

With Jess's arms wrapped around her, Hannah felt safer than she had since being a child nestled on her father's lap. Except for the fact that his firm chest and tender embrace made her toes curl. She needed to remember he was only here to fulfill a vow, nothing more. A good, kind soul who was tasked with taking care of her as a brother.

Jess tucked her head under his chin, and she closed her eyes. It was moments like this her stuttering pulse refused to cooperate. She took a deep breath, then pulled away. Remaining in his grasp would give him the wrong idea. And separation would help her think straight.

She frowned and patted her hair with trembling fingers. "Why do men think it's acceptable to intimidate women?"

He reached for her, then dropped his hand. "I don't think that guy is picky about gender. I saw the look in his eyes. He was considering whether to take me on."

A shaky laugh escaped. "He must have seen something to tell him that wasn't a good idea." She ducked her head. "I'm sorry you keep having to save me. First, the river and now this. You must think me a helpless ninny."

"On the contrary. You're a strong, brave woman, but we all need support. A friend in times of need."

Her heart fell, and she gave herself a mental slap. Of course, he considered her nothing more than a friend. As it should be, but the realization still brought disappointment. She huffed out a sigh and squared her shoulders. "Thanks for saying that. I guess I've been on my own for too long. Anyway, I looked for the paperwork from the purchase, but haven't found it yet. I was finishing in the root cellar when Asa showed up." She shuddered. "Can he really take me to court?"

"Why don't I make us some coffee, and we can talk about it?"

"I could use some." She walked to the kitchen and sank into one of the chairs by the table while he busied himself at the stove. "Is this your way of stalling?"

"What? No, but the conversation will be serious. I figure we can use the pick-me-up." He set the pot on the burner. "To answer your question—yes, he can really take you to court. But the judge can decide to throw out the case for lack of evidence."

Her stomach clenched. "Do you think he has any?"

"I doubt it. That's why he tried scaring Quinn and then you with the vandalism. And why he showed up today. But I'll be honest; without the purchase receipt or the deed, he might win. When I was in town, I went to the town offices. They have no record of Quinn registering his deed with them. It's a long shot, but do you know where Mrs. Webb would have gone after selling?"

Hannah raised her gaze to Jess and shook her head. "Frankly, I was lucky to get her name. Like I said, Quinn held his business close to the vest. She could be anywhere. How are we going to find her? If we can't locate her, Asa may win."

"Not on my watch." He poured the coffee and set a mug in front of her before lowering himself in the chair across the table. "Besides, if he's the one who killed Quinn, he'll be going to jail, not panning for gold."

"What if the sheriff can't prove him guilty? Crimes go unsolved all the time."

"Maybe in the cities, but not Dahlonega, Georgia. Someone must have seen something. We'll just have to keep looking." He sipped the dark brew. "I've got some money set aside. We can hire a bounty hunter or someone like that to search for Mrs. Webb. Those kind of men are used to turning over rocks to find people who don't want to be found, and she's not hiding."

"That's a wonderful idea, but I can't let you pay for it. I've got money."

"Fair enough. Tomorrow, we'll head into town and see if the sheriff can recommend someone for the job."

Jess swallowed a grin. The feisty, independent woman he knew was back, refusing to let him pay for the investigation. After her tears, he was glad to see her spirit return. Was an outsider the best use of her money, or should he make the trek to find Mrs. Webb? Hannah would never agree to staying in town if he left, and she'd be in danger remaining at the cabin alone. Was there a trustworthy couple who would take her in? Would she be willing to bunk with them? Probably not. Besides, someone needed to take care of the animals.

He raked his fingers through his hair. Too many issues and not enough options. Apparently, they'd need to rely on a bounty hunter to get the job done. With any luck, the man wouldn't take too long to find the widow.

Why hadn't Quinn included Hannah in his plans? What man doesn't talk to his wife about the financial aspect of their lives? Was Quinn intentionally secretive, hiding shady dealings? Probably not. His own father took care of the bills, and his mother handled the household, using an allotment of money budgeted for staff and supplies. Would Mother know what to do if Father died, or would another man enter the picture to ensure she was provided for? What an archaic system.

"Are you okay?" Hannah's voice broke his reverie.

"Yeah, sorry. I got caught up in thinking about the logistics of finding this woman. I'd like to save you some money by going myself, but the bounty hunter will probably do a faster job of it, and I haven't finished the repairs." He winked, enjoying the flush his gesture brought to her cheeks. "Gotta earn my keep."

"You've already done more than enough, but I must admit I'm pleased with the improvements." Her eyebrows drew together. "I'd hate to leave such a nice place for Asa. Maybe you should hold off on doing more work."

"If you insist, but I don't think you have anything to worry about. Like I said, if he had proof of ownership, he'd be a lot less underhanded."

"I wish I had your confidence."

"I have enough for both of us." Yeah, right. *Lord, please take care of this situation. It's bad enough Hannah lost her husband, but are You going to take her livelihood, too? Help us find Mrs. Webb so we can set things straight with this Bennett guy. Keep us safe from harm and foil his plans. I want to believe everything is going to turn out all right, but I'm a bit like that guy in the Bible who said "I believe; help my unbelief." That's kind of where I am right now.*

"That means a lot to me." Her face lit up, and she sipped her coffee. Her lips twisted. "I let it get cold. I don't suppose there's more where that came from."

With a chuckle, he rose and grabbed her mug. "Sure. Then I'll rustle up some lunch. Tossing that guy out on his ear has given me an appetite."

Hannah snorted a laugh, then covered her mouth with one hand. Her eyes sparkled.

Steps light, he set down the fresh cup of coffee in front of her and returned to the stove. He needed to make her laugh more often. She'd been dealt a bad hand, and the sorrow had to be overwhelming some days, to say nothing of the stress associated with this Bennett guy. Yes, he definitely needed to focus on bringing a smile to her lips.

Her hand touched the small of his back, and he nearly leapt out of his boots. When had she gotten out of her chair? He tightened his grip on the fry pan, trying to pretend the feel of her fingers hadn't shot a buzzing sensation from his head to his toes. "Can I get you something?"

"I thought the least I could do was set the table for us."

"Oh, thanks." He rolled his eyes at his schoolboy response and tried to ignore the tingling on his skin. So much for remaining aloof.

Chapter Twelve

Hannah's stomach rumbled as she collected her tools. By the look of the sun, it was late afternoon, but the day had been her most unproductive since Quinn's death, so she was calling it quits. The muscles in her back protested with every movement, and her fingers ached to the bone. She trudged toward Fern and tucked the items into the pony's saddlebags.

Fern snorted and bobbed her head as if to say she was ready to get home, too. Hannah stroked her neck. "Good girl. I'll give you an extra rasher of oats tonight, then we'll all turn in early. Tomorrow is another day. Perhaps we'll collect more than a few handfuls of flakes."

Was the vein playing out? Should she hand the claim over to Mr. Bennett. He'd been conspicuously absent since Jess had thrown him out of her cabin two weeks ago. Was he plotting revenge, or had Jess put the fear of God in the man? Probably not; he'd seemed more angry than scared when he stomped from her place. She blew out a sigh and smoothed her hair. Good thing she didn't have a mirror to see her appearance.

Jess managed to look more rugged at the end of a full day of panning, whereas she looked disheveled and wan even after hours in the sun. She was tired of waiting. Waiting to see if Asa would pull some stunt against her. Waiting to see if the bounty hunter Jess had hired on her behalf found Mrs. Webb. Waiting to see if the sheriff determined the identity of Quinn's killer.

On the one hand, she wanted her problems solved. She needed closure even if it meant she lost the claim or discovered some terrible secret about her husband that caused his death. On the other, she wasn't ready to see Jess ride away on the back of his horse. She'd grown used to his steady presence.

She peeked over her shoulder at him as he packed his saddlebags. His hat was pushed back on his head, allowing the sun to light his face. Even from a distance, she could see the sparkle in his eyes. Nothing rattled him. He remained alert, but his vigilance held no fear. He treated her with respect and seemed to know when she needed a pick-me-up. Like today.

Yesterday, he'd used some of the last dried blueberries to make happy-face pancakes for breakfast, as if she were a child, but the gesture had brought a smile. She turned back to the pony before he caught her mooning at him like a lovestruck schoolgirl.

"I'll meet you back at the cabin." She swung onto the pony. "I want to get started on the evening chores." Without waiting for a reply, she wheeled the animal toward the trail that led home.

She eased the horse into a canter. "When all is said and done, Fern, it might just be you and me. How does that sound? Just us gals." She shook her head. If anyone saw her talking to the pony, they'd think she'd gone loco. Maybe she had, but the animal never offered an unsolicited opinion or tried to tell Hannah what was best. "What will our lives hold, girl? The claim has done well, and I've saved a decent amount of money. Even if I never collect enough to fulfill all my dreams, I can take care of myself for a long while."

Fern nickered as if in agreement, and Hannah giggled.

"There's more to life than money, Fern, but having it does set the mind at ease. One less worry, if you know what I mean. Where do you want to go when we're done with the claim? I've not been out of Georgia. You want to do a little traveling, girl?"

Hoofbeats sounded behind her, and Major whinnied a greeting. Jess chuckled. "For someone who wants to get a jump on chores, you sure are lollygagging."

She opened her mouth to protest, but he nudged his horse into a gallop and disappeared up the trail. Her words died in her throat, and she snickered. Yep, he knew just how to lighten her mood. She pressed her knees against Fern's sides, and the horse surged forward, apparently just as eager as Hannah to return home.

The trees cleared, and the cabin came into view. Despite the difficult memories, she did love the cozy, little house. How much longer would she remain? Until the claim dried up, or would Asa Bennett have his way before that occurred? Or would she tire of the back-breaking work and walk away on her own accord? How much gold was enough?

"I think too much, Fern."

Hannah slid from the horse, caressed the animal's muzzle, then led her toward the barn. Chickens clucked, begging to be fed. "All right, ladies. Give me a few minutes to rub down Fern. You'll get your dinner." Great, now she was talking to the chickens as well. She really had lost her mind.

She ducked into the dim barn and headed to Major's stall. Jess stood next to the stallion, his head bent over some sort of document. A letter? Her heart leapt. Had he heard from the bounty hunter?

As she approached, his head jerked toward her, and he folded the paper, then stuffed it into his pocket. "Caught up with me, I see. It's about time." His smile seemed forced.

"Ha, I let you win." Her stomach tightened. Why hadn't he mentioned the letter? Should she? What was he hiding? She shivered. And why was he concealing it?

Chapter Thirteen

"You go on thinking that." Jess forced a smiled as he studied Hannah's face. Her narrowed eyes and clenched jaws told him she was angry, suspicious, or both. She'd seen him put away the paper, but she'd not asked about it. Did she think it pertained to her? "Listen, I can put up the horses, if you want to get off your feet. It's been a disappointing day. You must be tired."

She lifted her chin. "No more than you." Spine stiff, she uncinched the pony's saddle and hung it on the railing, then removed the bit and bridle. She whispered a running monologue to the animal he couldn't hear. She'd obviously dismissed him, so he turned to Major with a frown.

Granted, the day had been a difficult, but did she have to take her foul mood out on him? Or did she expect him to share everything and was upset he hadn't? If he lived a hundred years, he'd never understand women.

They worked without talking, the only noises being the snuffling horses and the chickens who scratched and pecked the ground at their feet.

Jess curry-combed Major, and the tension slipped from his shoulders with the repetitive motion of pulling the stiff-bristled brush over the stallion's flank.

Was the claim played out? Surely, one poor day of panning didn't mean all the gold had been mined. How long did prospectors work an area before giving up and moving on? As the day progressed and the discoveries of the eyelash-sized flakes fewer and farther between, Hannah's posture became more determined. She dug with a vengeance, and her eyes took on a steely glint. She'd barely stopped for lunch, then snarled when he tried to encourage her.

If he talked to the other men to figure out whether her claim had gone bust, word would spread like wildfire on a summer day. Would the sheriff know, or would asking the lawman cause a problem for Hannah? Jess nibbled on the inside of his cheek. Too many questions and not enough answers.

Major whinnied and bobbed his head as if he could read Jess's mind and agreed with him. Jess chuckled and patted the horse's neck. "Thanks for the support, old man." He glanced over his shoulder at Hannah who had finished with Fern and was now feeding the chickens. Would she think he'd gone loco?

He hung the brush on a hook, then checked the horse's feet and legs for any problems. Seeing none, he grabbed the scoop and dumped oats into the trough. Major snorted and began to munch on his feed. "Yeah, it's about time I fed you, I know." Jess patted the horse again, then crossed his arms and watched him eat. Oh, to have the simple life of a horse.

"I'll be inside." Hannah's voice echoed in the barn. "No need to hurry."

"Okay. I may putter a bit out here."

Her footsteps faded, and he grimaced. She'd made her feelings clear—stay out from underfoot. Fine. There was plenty of work to be done in the barn, and the physicality of accomplishing something today would go a long way.

If the claim was dry, her problems might be solved. He didn't know the current state of her finances, but if Quinn had been making regular runs to the bank like she'd indicated, there must be a tidy sum built up. She could sell the property to the Bennett fellow, add the proceeds to her stash, and move on.

He winced, then marched to the back of the barn where he'd tucked the wood for the rocking chair. Unloading a washed-up claim to an unsuspecting man wasn't exactly the Christian thing to do. But was the claim really done producing? And when would that bounty hunter come through with Mrs. Webb? Hannah couldn't dispose of the property without proof she was the owner. But if she was able to sell sooner rather than later, Bennett should be able to find some gold. And then she'd be gone.

No need to follow that line of thinking yet. With a hard tug, he dragged out the boards and began to measure. Time passed, and he hummed as he labored. He'd forgotten how much he enjoyed working with wood. Cutting and shaping until an object of beauty emerged. He rubbed his palm against the smooth timber and smiled. Even if she did leave, she'd have something to remember him by.

Sunlight barely peeked through the barn slats, and he was squinting to see. Daytime was getting on, and Hannah must be starving by now. If he was late with making dinner, she'd have another reason to be irritated at him. He climbed to his feet and tossed a canvas over the pile. Fortunately, she didn't seem to be curious about the stack. The paper in his pocket crinkled as he moved. Should he tell her what the document contained?

"Jess?"

He strode into the center of the barn. "Yeah, I'm sorry. I got caught up with a project. I'll wash my hands and make dinner."

She stood with her hands on her hips, the frown on her face evident even in the dimness. "That's not why I'm out here. I've got a vegetable soup going on the stove." She huffed a breath, then pulled on one earlobe. "I'm finding out that Quinn had secrets. Lots of secrets, and I'm trying not to be upset about this, but it was all I could think about while I was preparing the food. And I think we need to talk about it. If this partnership is going to work, we need to be open with each other."

His mind raced. She was going to ask about the paper. He gave her what he hoped was an open and encouraging smile. "Okay. What would you like to know?"

"What did you put in your pocket earlier? You looked as guilty as a little boy with his hand in the cookie jar. If the paper is about me, I have a right to know what's on it. I don't need another man keeping secrets in some false sense of protection. Did you hear from the bounty hunter? It can't be the deed. You would have told me that."

"I'm not withholding information about your claim or your case." *Forgive me, Lord.* The paper is nothing you need to be concerned about."

He tried not to squirm while she studied his face for a long moment. If she ever decided to take up teaching, she had the schoolmarm glare perfected.

"I can't believe you're not going to tell me what it is. You're obviously hiding something, just like every other man in my life not telling me stuff." She jerked her head toward the house. "Soup's probably ready by now, but in the morning I'd like you to pack up and head out. I don't need someone here I can't trust." She whirled on her heel and marched from the barn.

Jess rubbed the back of his neck. He couldn't leave. Not yet. He had to find a way to make amends so she'd let him stay. Judging from her expression, he had his work cut out for him.

Chapter Fourteen

Hunched over the table, Hannah spooned vegetable soup into her mouth. Her stomach protested, but she continued to eat. She refused to let the situation with Jess ruin her appetite. The day had been bad enough; ending it on a sour note with Quinn's friend was her fault. He'd been nothing but kind and helpful since his arrival. Why had she assumed he was being underhanded? She frowned. Because he'd looked guilty when he shoved the paper out of sight.

She was never one for needing lots of girlfriends to jaw with, but she could use one now. First, she found herself talking to the pony, and now she was talking to herself. Pathetic. With no brothers and very few boys her age at the church her family attended, her experience with men was limited. She'd been enthralled when Quinn had shown up. He was handsome and sophisticated, and she fell for him. Hard. Then been stunned when he'd chosen her out of all the other girls. Their courtship had been short, and they were married after only six months. Would things have turned out differently if they'd had more time to get acquainted?

Pushing away the empty bowl, she slumped in the chair. Only five weeks had passed since his death. She was supposed to be mourning him, yet all she could remember were the difficulties, the growing apart that marked their marriage. Nearly ten years together, yet she felt like she barely knew him. How could she grieve a stranger?

Maybe their distant relationship was her fault. Perhaps her expectations were too high. Her parents' deep love was evident. Occasional differences arose, but Mother and Father resolved them before retiring for the night. They never went to bed angry. She'd tried to model her behaviors after her mother's, so the first time she and Quinn argued, she'd followed him around the house demanding a resolution. He'd alternately sulked and yelled at her, finally leaving the house and not returning until morning. As a result, whenever they disagreed, she swallowed her hurt and disappointment.

"Stop wallowing in the past." Hannah pressed her lips together and climbed to her feet, taking her cup and bowl to the sink. She heated some water, then poured it into the basin and scrubbed the dishes. She glanced at the pot of soup.

Was Jess like Quinn? Would he brood and give her the silent treatment, skipping dinner so he didn't have to see her or address their conflict? With another sigh, she dried the dishes and put them away. What if he accepted her order to leave? She'd gotten used to his easy presence, but it was obviously just a façade. Good thing she'd discovered his true nature before too much time had passed.

The door opened, and Jess stepped into the house, his frame filling the tiny cabin. Her pulse skipped, and her hands trembled, so she busied them by grabbing a bowl and filling it with soup. She set it on the table with a thump. "This is all we have. I didn't make any biscuits." Another failure.

"Smells divine. Thanks for rustling up some grub." He strode across the room and dropped into one of the chairs, then gestured to the other. "Please join me. I'd like to talk about what happened. I want to clear the air."

She gaped at him for a long moment, then hurried to sit down. He was nothing like Quinn. Tucking her hands in her lap, she crossed her ankles. She'd wait for him to speak.

After his first bite, he moaned. "Fantastic." He ate several more mouthfuls, then put down his spoon and wiped his mouth. "That took the edge off, but I'll finish after things are square between us."

He leaned forward. "I'm sorry you don't think you can trust me. We seem so comfortable that I forget I've only been here a month or so. Not nearly long enough to understand each other too well." He rolled his eyes. "To say nothing of our personal histories. I know I'm trustworthy, so I assume you know it, too. Foolish. Anyway, I'd like for us to start over."

Hannah licked her lips. A pretty speech, but was he genuine, or was he trying to make her forget about the paper? She searched his face, and he seemed willing to let her do so. A gentle smile clung to his lips; his eyes were clear and steady. Either he was a better actor than those she'd seen on the stage in Atlanta, or he was being honest with her. "I'd like to believe you. You're right about how we get along, and I like having you here." Her face warmed, but she pressed on. "It's nice having someone I can count on, but you need to tell me something. Wouldn't you expect me to prove myself to you if you had doubts?"

"Yes." He grinned. "I guess I should have brought character references."

"You thought Quinn would be here to welcome you."

"True." Jess laced his fingers. "And I'm sorry he wasn't. I'm sorry you've experienced this terrible tragedy. No one should have to lose their spouse to violence."

"But as a fallen world, bad things are going to happen." She shrugged. "And sometimes they're going to happen to good people. We may not understand why God lets them happen, but—"

His eyebrow lifted. "Are you back on speaking terms with Him?"

She ducked her head. "I'm still struggling, but I no longer blame Him for what happened."

"I'm happy for you. I'll continue to pray."

Hannah raised her gaze to his. "Then you say things like that, and I wonder if I should trust you."

"Look. I know I messed up when I refused to tell you what the paper was. I still can't tell you specifically, but you will find out eventually. It's not a secret. It's a surprise. A wonderful surprise." He pinched together his thumb and index finger and ran them across his mouth, his eyes twinkling. "And that's all I'm going to say. You'll just have to wait to find out."

"A surprise?" The tightness in her chest eased, and her pulse tripped. What could he being doing for her that would bring such pleasure to his face? "How long do I have to wait?"

Jess burst out laughing. "So, we're okay now?"

She giggled and nodded, trying to ignore the feelings of giddiness.

Chapter Fifteen

The sun was barely over the horizon when Hannah slipped from bed, dragged on her clothes, and poked her feet into her boots. She brushed her hair and braided it into one long rope that hung down her back. Perhaps today they would finally unearth a decent amount of gold. The week had been nearly fruitless, working almost ten hours each day until they had to put their faces inches from the pan to determine if any flakes nestled amid the sand.

Lifting her chin, she sniffed the air. The aroma of coffee mingled with the enticing scent of eggs, bacon, and biscuits. Her stomach rumbled in response, and she smiled. Taking a last peek in the mirror, she nodded, then berated herself for caring about her appearance. She opened the door and clomped into the kitchen, then froze at the sight of him.

Dressed in his usual jeans, cotton shirt, and boots, he'd tied one of her aprons around his waist. His hair stuck up in several directions as if he'd forgotten to comb it. A smudge of flour was stark against his tanned cheek. He turned, and a lazy grin curled his lips. "Good morning, sleepyhead."

Her breath caught, then she blinked and forced herself to move forward. "Sleepyhead? It's not much past six o'clock. What's got you so chipper?" She winced at the edge in her voice.

"Someone needs her coffee." He filled a cup, then presented it to her with a bow.

Hannah reached for the cup, and their fingers grazed. Her eyes widened as a jolt shot down her arm all the way to her elbow. Did he feel that, or was she imagining things? Cradling the heavy mug with both hands, she took a tentative sip of the fragrant brew. Flavor burst in her mouth, and she sighed.

He chuckled. "Better?"

"Much." She dropped into one of the kitchen chairs. "Sorry for being cranky this morning."

"No need to apologize." He returned to the stove, dished their food, then set the plates on the table. He reached for her hands. "I'll say the blessing."

Like he always did. She nibbled her lower lip as she placed her fingers in his and bowed her head. One of these days she'd rustle up the nerve to say grace, but her renewed relationship with God was still rusty. Although expected, the tingle of his skin against hers sent a shiver up her spine. Maybe she needed to pray about that, too.

Jess kept up a running dialogue, and she appreciated his efforts to lighten her mood. He was a good man. Too good.

They ate quickly, saddled the horses, and headed to the claim, the crisp sunrise heralding a clear day. A rabbit bounded across their path, and squirrels chattered in the branches overhead. Hannah took a deep breath, filling her lungs with cool mountain air. As they drew closer to the claim, the murmur of conversation reached her ears. Apparently, she and Jess weren't the only miners to get a jump on the day.

The trees cleared, and the river came into view. Crawling with men, the water bubbled and rushed over the rocks. How many more weeks before the spring thaw slowed the flow to a trickle? She shook her head to clear the morose thoughts.

Jess glanced over, and his teeth flashed as he gave her a broad smile. "Today is the day. I can feel it in my bones."

At the look of sheer joy on his face, she grinned. His mood was infectious, and her heart lightened. *Thank You, Father, for sending Jess to help me. Especially for helping me find You again.* She climbed out of the saddle and hobbled the pony at the edge of the clearing. She unpacked her tools and carried them to the riverbank. Behind her, Jess whistled a slightly off-key version of "Amazing Grace." He hit a particularly strident note, and she cringed. Did he not hear that?

His tools clanked as he approached and kneeled close by. A breeze wafted his scent toward her, a mixture of bacon, leather, and the essence she'd come to associate with him. She gulped and shifted to her right, then pushed her trowel into the sandy bottom of the river. Scoop. Swirl. Tip. Swirl. Pick. Repeat. Except there was nothing to pick. No curved golden flakes nestled in the sand. And certainly no nuggets. She huffed out a sigh.

"I heard that." He scooted over to her. "Remember today is the day." His breath tickled her cheek.

Her stomach buzzed as if hornets swarmed inside, and she glanced at him, then put two trembling fingers to her forehead in a mock salute. "Right. I forgot."

With a smirk, he nudged her shoulder, and she snickered. She'd get whiplash if her mood continued to ricochet by the second. Hannah ducked her head and resumed panning. Scoop. Swirl. Tip. Swirl. Nothing.

Jess rose and walked to her right, then shoved his trowel between a pair of rocks and poured the soil into his pan. She watched him from the corner of her eye. His technique had improved over the weeks, and he was almost as proficient as the other miners. His muscles bunched under his shirt, and her mouth dried. She gave herself a mental slap and turned her attention back to her pan.

He yelped as if bitten and jumped to his feet.

Her head whipped toward him. "What? Are you okay? What happened?"

"Just fine." He grinned like a drunken sailor and waved his pan at her. "Found me some gold."

"A flake or two doesn't mean anything."

"Exactly. Which is why I'm so happy about this nugget."

Her pulse raced as she grabbed his arm. "A nugget? Stop moving that thing."

"Sorry." His eyes danced. "I got caught up in the moment."

The sun slipped from behind a cloud and glinted off the chunk of yellow ore. Hannah snatched the nugget from the pan, the metal cold against her palm. She chortled. Was the drought over?

He dropped the pan, then grabbed her in a bear hug and lifted her off feet.

Her hat dropped to the ground as her arms slipped around his neck.

"Well, isn't this cozy?"

Sheriff Fawley's sardonic tones doused her excitement, and her face flamed. Jess released her, and she bent to pick up her Stetson. She schooled her features, then straightened and looked him in the eye. "Do you have news?"

He frowned from atop his horse. "Not very appropriate behavior for a new widow, Hannah. And you ought to know better, too, Mr. Vogel."

Hannah gritted her teeth as her temper flared, and Jess stiffened beside her. "Mind your business, Sheriff. We weren't doing anything wrong. Just celebrating."

"Men and women don't hug in public, and you know it."

She waved her hand in a dismissive gesture. "Please say what you've come to tell me, and then you can be on your way and not have to be offended."

"Fine." He crossed his arms. "The law is a bit murky about you owning this claim."

"What?" She gaped at him. "Quinn left me all his worldly goods. I've got the will to prove it."

"That might be the case, but women in Georgia aren't generally allowed to own property, and this claim is considered property." He rubbed his jaw and looked smug. "I happen to know Asa Bennett is intent on pressing his case, but if you married I could convince him to move along and stop pestering you. And you'd keep your reputation intact. You know people are starting to talk about the fact this Vogel fellow is living with you."

"He's not living with me! And people need to mind their own business." She shook her head. "And I haven't changed my mind about marrying you, Sheriff. It's a kind offer, really, but I'm not sure marrying you is the right answer." She peeked at Jess out of the corner of her eye. He stood ramrod straight, and the vein on his temple pulsed. Kudos to him for letting her handle the situation, when it appeared he'd like to knock the sheriff off his horse. She cleared her throat. "Besides, we're expecting to hear from Mrs. Webb any day."

"Suit yourself, but I won't be able to protect you from slick lawyers if we're not hitched."

"I know." She tugged at her bottom lip. She didn't want to be in a loveless relationship, but what if he was right and she'd lose the claim without a husband. "Give me a couple of days to think on it."

"Fine, but don't take too long." He sent one more thunderous scowl at Jess, then yanked on the horse's reins and trotted down the path.

"I didn't mean to get you into trouble, Hannah." Jess scuffed his boot in the dirt. "I shouldn't have grabbed you."

"Ridiculous, Jess. We're friends, and if people aren't willing to understand that, then I have no time for them. I get kind of fed up with worrying about the rules." She gestured to the men along the riverbank. "And this isn't exactly high society."

"You're right, but once sullied, a woman's reputation is difficult to regain. And that could prove to be an impedance should you decide not to marry the sheriff."

She frowned. Why did a woman's fate depend on a man?

Chapter Sixteen

A pair of crows squawked overhead as the sheriff disappeared into the trees. Jess grimaced and tugged his hat low on his forehead. The burning sensation in his stomach threatened to bring back his breakfast. Did the lawman really expect Hannah to accept his proposal? And why make it? His attitude gave no indication that he actually cared for the young widow. Was he hoping to get his hands on her gold?

Shoulders stiff, she stuffed the nugget into her pocket. "Guess we better do some panning now that the claim seems to be producing again." She trudged to the riverbank and crouched near the water.

Jess fisted his hands. The man seemed downright smug when he announced the possibility that Hannah might not have a right to the inheritance. Everyone seemed to forget only a few weeks had passed since the poor woman had been widowed. She was still grieving and would be for a while. The sheriff should have at least mentioned her loss before trying to railroad her into a wedding.

But was the man right? Was securing a husband the only way Hannah could hang on to the claim? He knew nothing about inheritance laws so would be hard pressed to refute the sheriff's assertion. Shouldn't the man be out looking for a killer instead of getting involved in her legal issues?

He straightened his spine and marched to the water's edge. The sun glinted off the braid that hung down Hannah's back. She somehow managed to look feminine and pretty in her jeans and flannel shirt rather than boyish. Perhaps it was the graceful curve of her neck or her smooth, porcelain complexion. His mouth dried, and he huffed out a breath. He was here to take care of her, not ogle as if he were some greenhorn cowboy who'd never seen a girl, but if he were honest, she'd begun to mean more to him than he wanted to admit.

Take care of her. He snapped his fingers. Before he could change his mind, he blurted, "Hannah, you could marry me."

The crows cackled again, and his face flamed. Was God trying to tell him the idea was a bad one?

Cheeks pink, Hannah narrowed her eyes. "What did you say?"

"I...uh...said you could marry me. Instead of the sheriff. If you need a husband."

Myriad emotions danced across her face. "Why would you offer?"

"I promised Quinn I'd take care of you if anything happened to him. And it seems the vultures are circling."

"You think Sheriff Fawley is up to no good? I've known him a lot longer than you. Convince me your offer isn't a way to do me out of my property."

He jutted out his chin. "We've been over this before. I don't want your money. I'm trying to protect your inheritance, and it sounds like Georgia law might not cooperate if you remain single, no matter what Quinn's will says. If you don't trust me, we can go to a lawyer and get him to draw up papers that prevent me from getting my hands on your money."

She pulled her lower lip under her teeth as she studied him. "You've got all the answers, don't you?"

"Nope. I'm trying to give you some options, and one choice would be to marry a friend of your husband's. A friend Quinn trusted enough to contact and ask for help. Maybe that's a recommendation. Maybe it's not, I don't know." He shrugged. "This day sure isn't turning out like I thought it would. Listen, there are plenty of miners here. If you'd rather I headed back to the cabin and give you some space, I'd be happy to get some chores done."

Shaking her head, she handed him a pan. "No, stay and help me mine. Your offer surprised me. I guess I overreacted. I trust you." She ducked her head. "But I'm not sure I want to marry you. I'll think on it while I'm considering the sheriff's proposition."

Jess grabbed the pan. "Must be tough to have multiple men asking for your hand."

Batting her eyelashes, she grinned. "You have no idea how difficult it is to be so sought after."

He chuckled, then squeezed her shoulder. "I'm proud of you, Hannah. You're a strong women and have held up well considering everything that's happened. Please know that my...uh...proposal to wed doesn't mean I expect physicality...at least not right off. You've only just lost your husband, and this would be a marriage in name only until you're ready."

"I appreciate your candor, Jess. That means a lot." Her face was scarlet. "But I don't want to rush this decision, so you need to give me some time."

"Absolutely." He cleared his throat. "And no matter what you decide, I'll remain and help you as long as you need me. I made a promise I intend to keep."

"Okay." She gave him a tentative smile before plunging her shovel into the sand and dumping the silt into her pan.

Heart hammering in his chest, Jess shoved his trowel between a cluster of rocks. What if she didn't choose him? Or worse. Accepted the sheriff's proposal. The man would run him out of town in a flash, and he couldn't let that happen. He needed to convince Hannah to pick him.

Jess nudged her shoulder. "You realize I'm the best choice."

Her lips twisted. "We're not talking about this right now."

"I know." He grinned and puffed out his chest. "I'm just giving you fair warning that I'm going to do whatever it takes for you to select me."

"Thanks for the warning." She giggled and swatted him. "Now, get back to work. We've got gold to find."

With two fingers to the brim of his hat, he gave her an exaggerated salute. "Whatever you say, boss."

Her laughter rang out like silver bells.

Yep, he planned to win this challenge so he could spend the rest of his life making her smile.

Chapter Seventeen

Hannah pushed away her dinner plate, then swallowed the last of her water. She sent him a saucy smile. "Delicious, Jess. You'll make some lucky girl a wonderful wife one day."

He chuckled and picked up their soiled dishes. "I told you this afternoon. You'll be saying yes. Now, it's your turn to wash up, but I'll give you a hand since you were so complimentary." He set the dinnerware into the sink, then picked up a drying cloth.

Her heart skipped. She was treading in dangerous territory. "And I told you and the sheriff I'm not inclined to marry." She rose and went to the stove where she grabbed the pot of water she'd heated before dinner and poured it into the sink. She rubbed the chunk of soap against a cloth and began to scrub one of the plates.

She handed him the clean dish, and their hands grazed. Her fingers tingled, and she plunged them back into the water. Definitely dangerous territory. She cleared her throat. "You've told me about your life after the war, but what about before? Have you always worked farms?"

"It's one of the few things I'm good at."

"You underestimate yourself. Don't forget the repairs. You've done a beautiful job replacing the rotting boards, and improving the barn."

He shrugged. "That's just part of farmwork."

"And you're very good at it." She washed another plate and set it on the counter to avoid the risk of contact. "What's your favorite part of farmwork?"

"That's a tough question. There's great satisfaction in all of it. Standing at the end of a field that's been fully plowed and seeing the rich dirt waiting for seed is incredibly satisfying. Months later, harvesting the abundance knowing you did your best but recognizing that without God as your partner sending the rain and sunshine, you wouldn't have anything, is humbling. I love caring for the animals. They're dependent on you, and if you're good to them, they'll give you their all." He flushed. "Didn't mean to go on like that."

"You're passionate about working the land. Not all men are like that. They farm because they have to or because it's the only job they know." She smiled. "I appreciate you setting it aside for a season to help me. Knowing how much you enjoy farming makes your coming here even more special, and I thank you."

The red in his cheeks deepened. "I'm enjoying the panning. More than I thought I would. And you could say I'm still working the land, but I'm harvesting gold rather than produce. It's been interesting to see the earth from a different perspective, as producing minerals rather than food."

"You sound like a scientist now." She picked up the skillet and dunked it into the tepid water, then poured in more hot water from the pot.

Rolling the towel, he thwacked her arm with the linen. "Now you're making fun of me."

She squealed and flicked water at him.

He held up his hands in surrender. "Okay, let's quit this before we get into trouble."

"Fair enough." She sobered up. "Do you ever think about your time during the war? Occasionally, Quinn had nightmares, and he'd wake up shouting, sometimes crying."

"War takes a terrible toll on men. We see things no one should ever have to look at. I understand why we went to war. We were reasserting our independence from Britain, but the battles were awful, and I hope our future leaders will find ways to settle their differences through some other means. But I fear that won't be the case. The Bible says we'll always have wars."

"It seems you're right. The US has been fighting the Natives off and on for years."

"We keep taking their land. It's unsurprising they resist." He put away the plates. "What about you? After you buy all that land and build your library, what are you going to do? Buy another gold claim?"

"Not more gold. I'm not getting any younger, you know." She tilted her head. "Maybe raise animals, you know, cows and chickens, or horses." She shook her head. "I'd be no good at farming, but I do like the animals."

An image of a farmhouse perched on a knoll popped into her mind. Rustic, but comfortable with a wide wraparound porch that held a bunch of rocking chairs. Sturdy chairs. Not like the rickety one that was going to collapse one of these days. Two fireplaces. She hated being cold, and two hearths would ensure she was warm no matter what the temperature outside.

She'd sit on the porch and look over the fenced-in fields filled with magnificent horses that men would come from miles around to purchase. She'd be known as a purveyor of fine stallions and mares. Visions of rolling green hills swam in front of her. The door to her imaginary house opened, and Jess stepped outside, his handsome features tanned from working their herd. She hissed in a breath. What happened to not getting married?

"You okay?"

"Yeah." She ducked her head. "Just thinking nonsense."

"Care to share?" He narrowed his eyes.

"Nope." She grabbed a chair and dragged it to the counter. She climbed on the seat and reached for the cups.

"Hey, I can put away that stuff."

"I've got them." She tucked the pewter vessels into the cupboard, then stepped down. The chair tipped, and her arms flailed. She fell against Jess, her breath whooshing from her lungs. His arms came around her, and she froze, pressed against his firm chest. Cheeks scorching, she looked up at him. "How clumsy of me. I'm so sorry."

His face was inches from hers, his hands warm on her back through the thin fabric of her cotton shirt. "You need to be more careful." His voice was low and seemed to catch in his throat. His pupils dilated making his chocolate-brown eyes nearly black.

Heart hammering against her ribs, she nodded. Her mouth went dry, and she licked her lips.

Jess's gaze flicked to her mouth, then he lowered his head and kissed her.

Her toes curled, and a sigh escaped. Quinn's kisses never felt like this. Quinn! Less than two months had passed since he went into the grave, and she was kissing another man. One who made her heart sing, but it was much too soon. She had no right to care for another. She yanked herself from his arms and fled to the bedroom, slamming the door behind her.

She rushed to the mirror. Her flushed cheeks and sparkling eyes told her what she suspected. She was falling in love with Jess Vogel.

Chapter Eighteen

Pink and purple stripes of dawn barely pushed back the darkness as Hannah climbed out of bed and dragged on her clothes. Sleep eluded her most of the night, and her eyes burned with fatigue. She lit the lamp, the flame flaring as it caught. She poured water into the basin, then shivered as she washed her face. Daily temperatures reached into the sixties, but nights continued to hold a chill.

She clomped out of the bedroom and made her way to the kitchen. Rummaging in the bins, she frowned. The bread loaf was no more than a stub, and after all that happened yesterday, she'd forgotten to make more. Good thing she was up early.

Gathering her supplies, she smiled when she saw the pitcher of water on the counter. Jess never failed to ensure she had fresh water each morning. Even after last night's kiss that made her head spin, he had enough composure to fill the jug. She touched her lips. They felt the same, yet different.

How would he act this morning? His teasing last night had pushed away the clouds, making her laugh more than she had in months. The burden of worry had lightened for a short time, easing the heaviness that seem to hang on her shoulders like a wool cloak.

Then she'd stumbled into his arms. Her face warmed at the memory. It was bad enough she wore men's clothes while she was panning, but she'd exacerbated her lack of femininity by crashing into him like an oaf. Why had he kissed her? Surely, he didn't think she was attractive. Besides, he'd come as a favor to Quinn, so he couldn't have feelings for her.

With practiced motions, she combined the ingredients, then worked the dough into a smooth ball. Now, to let it rise. Her coffee wasn't nearly as flavorful as Jess's, but she desperately needed the pick-me-up offered by the dark brew.

Outside, dawn's fingers lightened the sky, outlining the trees. He should be up by now and tending to the animals. Time to get breakfast started. He'd spoiled her by doing most of the cooking, but at some point he'd be gone, and she'd have to fend for herself. Alone.

"Stop borrowing trouble, girl." Hannah huffed out a sigh. "Granny would say if you'd focus on your chores, there wouldn't be time to mope. And she would know. Crossing an ocean to settle in a new country as a newlywed, then raising six children as a widow during the Revolution. The woman had gumption. What would she say about Jess? Or the fact that Hannah had marriage proposals from two men? Would Granny tell her to pick one or forge ahead on her own like she'd done?

Hunched into his coat, Jess headed to the cabin. Hopefully, the sunrise would bring some heat to the day. By July, he'd be wishing for some coolness. He swung open the door, and the aromas of coffee, eggs, and ham greeted him. "Someone was up early."

Face flushed, Hannah smiled. "Yes, and it's only fair that I cook your breakfast. I've let you wait on me far too long." She poured his cup and handed it to him, her eyes sparkling even in the dim light.

He glanced at the table where she'd set plates, utensils, and cups. "What may I do to be helpful?"

"Just have a seat."

"You mean stay out of the way."

The pink on her cheeks deepened, and she giggled, a sound reminiscent of his mother's wind chimes.

His chest lightened, and he chuckled as he sat down. He'd wondered how she'd greet him this morning. After last night's kiss, she'd fled into the bedroom, and he'd waited for over an hour to see if she'd reappear. She'd remained hidden, so he'd gone to the barn and spent hours praying about what to do. The only word he kept getting from the Lord was patience. Not exactly his strong suit.

Sipping the coffee, he relished the warmth that spread from his stomach to his limbs. She puttered at the stove, dishing the food and checking the bread...the picture of domesticity. He could get used to this.

Hannah set down the plates, then dropped into the chair. "I used the last of the ham steaks, so we'll need to go into town for supplies soon."

"Good timing." He held out his hand, and she slipped her fingers into his. He said a quick blessing, and they dug into the food. "I've been thinking we should speak to the attorney and get his advice on how to proceed. He could tell us how long we should wait to hear from the bounty hunter. Asa Bennett seems intent on getting his hands on your claim, so we need to know how to combat that. I'm afraid we're running out of time." Jess downed his coffee, then rose to refill his cup. His time to woo Hannah was also slipping away. If he was able to solve her problems, perhaps she'd look at him in a different light. As a man with something more than a strong back to offer.

She held up her cup, and he topped off her drink. The smile she gave him was dazzling, and he nearly dropped the carafe. Returning the pot to the stove, he rolled his eyes. Smooth, Romeo, real smooth.

"That sounds good. Frankly, the idea of spending the day hunched over a pan holds no allure today. I guess I could use a break."

"Excellent." He polished off his breakfast, then stood. "I'll hitch the pony to the wagon."

"Give me a few minutes to wash the dishes, and I'll join you." She laid her hand on his arm. "Thank you for all you do around the house. I don't know how I could handle this without you."

His mouth dried, and the spot where her hand lay tingled. Tongue-tied, he nodded before rushing from the house. What was wrong with him this morning? He was as awkward as a schoolboy. "You know exactly what's wrong with you, old man. And you've got it bad."

An hour later, they crested the hill that took them into town, and Jess breathed a sigh of relief. Sitting next to Hannah on the buckboard had brought exquisite pain. Delight in her proximity and lighthearted conversation mingled with disappointment that she would probably choose the sheriff's proposal over his. She hadn't said anything specific, but her demeanor suggested she'd come to some sort of decision. Hopefully, she'd let him down easy.

They pulled up in front of the sheriff's office, and Jess helped her from the wagon, his hands remaining on her tiny waist a fraction too long. Fawley met them at the door, a scowl on his face. Now, what?

Jess's pulse raced as the entered the building, then sped up at the sight of the bounty hunter. He strode forward, arm outstretched. "We were beginning to wonder if we'd ever see you again."

The man took off his hat and bowed at Hannah. "Ma'am. I apologize for taking so long, but Mrs. Webb had taken ill and was not in a condition to meet with me until recently."

Hannah's hand flew to her throat. "Oh no. How awful for her. But she's recovering?"

"Yes, ma'am, and she sends her regards. Says if you ever get to Charleston, to look her up for a visit." He fumbled in his pocket. "She sent her copy of the sales receipt and deed as well as her original grant from the lottery."

With trembling fingers, she took the papers.

Jess stifled the desire to wrap his arm around her for support. That move would not endear him to the lawman. Instead, he peered over her shoulder. "Both your names are on the deed, Hannah. I don't think we need an attorney to tell us that's good news. Your ownership doesn't hinge on Quinn's will."

She brightened. "Wonderful. Now, we'll have something if Mr. Bennett takes us to court." She fanned her face with the documents. "I can't tell you what a relief this is."

The sheriff's scowl deepened. Was he realizing that Hannah wouldn't need to marry him? Jess's heart clenched. She wouldn't need him either.

Chapter Nineteen

Hannah stuffed the documents into her reticule and smiled at Jess. "Amazing how a couple of pieces of paper can change one's life."

"Indeed." He crooked his elbow. "How about if we grab an early lunch to celebrate."

"A wonderful idea." She grasped his arm and turned to Sheriff Fawley. "Would you like to join us?"

"Nah." He glowered at her. "I've got work to do. Remember, I still need to find your husband's killer."

She sensed his unspoken reprimand: that she had no right to enjoy herself while Quinn's murderer was on the loose. She raised her chin. She wouldn't let him see that his words stung. "I appreciate your efforts, Sheriff. Everything you've done to help me. I'll take my leave now."

With a tug on Jess's arm, she marched out the door. Once outside, she allowed her shoulders to slump. How exhausting to have to constantly prove oneself.

He patted her hand. "In his own way, he cares for you, and he's disappointed you may no longer need to marry him."

Her gaze shot to his face. "Cares for me? He has a funny way of showing it. All he's done since Quinn's death is boss me around. I don't need that kind of care."

"Don't let him get to you or ruin our festivities."

"You always know what to say." Her chin trembled, and she pressed her lips together. Why did she have to cry when she got angry? No wonder men thought she was weak.

They arrived at the restaurant, and he held the door open for her. Aware of his closeness, she slipped past him. He always made her feel important. Why couldn't more men act like him?

Kitty hurried toward them and embraced Hannah in a warm hug. "I haven't seen you since the funeral. How are you holding up?"

"There are good days and bad. But a friend of Quinn's from Atlanta is helping me, so I'm getting by. This is Jess Vogel."

"I'm so glad Hannah has someone. Is she actually letting you do anything? She's always so independent."

Jess chuckled. "That she is."

"Okay, you two, I'm right here and can hear you."

"Sorry, Hannah." Kitty didn't look the least bit apologetic.

"Yeah, right." Hannah poked the young woman and shook her head. "Can we get a table?"

"Sure. Right this way." She seated them near the window. "Cookie made some wonderful beef stew, or I can bring you a menu."

"Sounds great to me. Jess?"

"Make that two."

"Excellent, and I'll be right back with your coffee." With a swish of her skirt, Kitty wended her way through the tables and into the kitchen.

"She seems like a nice gal. How long have you known her?"

"Ever since we arrived. While Quinn was building the house, we stayed at the hotel and took most of our meals here." Hannah sighed. "I didn't realize how much I missed female companionship until I saw her."

Jess reached across the table and squeezed her hand. "You should take some time off. I can work the claim while you visit and do some fun things."

"I'm still in mourning, Jess." She extricated her hand. "Chet reminded me of that in the office."

"I don't want to make light of your loss, but living is the best way to honor Quinn. I don't know anything about your relationship, but would he expect you closet yourself away from others now that he's gone?"

"I doubt it, but society—"

"Has ridiculous rules, and as you've said before, Dahlonega isn't exactly a hotbed of culture."

Kitty returned with a tray that held two fragrant bowls of stew, steaming cups of coffee, and a basket filled with cornbread. She set the items down with a thump. "Enjoy, and there's plenty more where that came from, but save room for chess pie."

"Thanks, Kitty." Jess held up his hand. "And before we leave, Hannah's going to talk to you about getting together."

"Jess—"

The waitress grinned. "I think I like you, Mr. Vogel. You're going to be good for our Hannah." She patted Hannah's shoulder, then made her way to a table on the other side of the room where two elderly women in silk chatted, heads close together.

"You are incorrigible." Hannah shook her finger at Jess.

"Yes, but that's what makes me so endearing."

She snorted a laugh, then ducked her head, her cheeks burning.

He spooned some of the stew into his mouth, then moaned. "Best I've ever had. Eat up. You'll need your strength for the rest of the celebration."

Her head whipped up. "What do you have in mind?"

"Nope. You'll just have to wait and see." He cleared his throat. "All kidding aside, I'm pleased God chose to work this out for you. It was hard to be patient, and a positive outcome wasn't guaranteed, but He gave you the desires of your heart."

"He has been good to me which is more than I deserve considering I turned my back on Him for a while."

"None of us deserve His gifts and mercy. Good thing He loves us so much." Jess sipped his coffee. "How much longer will you work the claim? Until it plays out, or do you want to sell it at some point?"

"I am getting tired of the work. It's backbreaking." She glanced out the window and smiled at the sight of a young woman carrying a baby. "Until autumn, I think, maybe late summer. I'd like to find a place here in town so I don't have to build again. Having to manage a bunch of men who probably won't want to take direction from a woman makes me cringe. And I don't want you or the sheriff to have to handle it. Especially you. You've put your life on hold for long enough. I appreciate all you've done, but you need to be pursuing your own dreams."

The food sat like lead in her stomach at the thought of Jess leaving. She was glad she no longer had to marry to solve her problems, but she would have accepted his proposal. He was a fine man, but more than that, she loved him. She knew that now. But being in a marriage where she was the only one with feelings would have been excruciating. *Thank You, God, for working out my deed.*

Jess pushed aside his empty bowl, then wiped his mouth. "I'm proud of you for sticking to your guns, Hannah. Many women would have shriveled up or run at the first sign of difficulty."

She shrugged and waved her hand in a dismissive gesture.

"I mean it. You don't think of yourself as a strong woman, but you are. Did you learn that from your mother? Is she just as stubborn as you?"

She cradled the mug in her hands, and her eyes took on a distant glaze. "No, my Granny lived with us for the last ten years of her life. Everything I am is because of her. I don't know what happened in the privacy of her bedroom, but she always faced her challenges head-on. She lost my grandfather when her youngest child was only four years old. She never remarried."

"Wow. She sounds indomitable."

"She was." A sheen of moisture formed in her eyes. "I still miss her."

"I'll bet she's proud of you, too."

"I hope so." She ran her finger around the rim of the cup, then looked up with a smile. "She'd have loved panning for gold. And she'd have the other miners eating out of her hand. It's hard to describe, but she wasn't flirty, but she was so generous that people fell over themselves to give back to her."

"Money?"

"No. Of herself and her time. No matter how busy she was, she'd take the time to talk to whomever she ran into. And she could always tell if someone was struggling, even if they didn't say anything."

"She sounds like a very special woman." He tilted his head. "You think she'd wear jeans like you do? Or would she try to manage in her skirts?"

Hannah chortled. "I can't imagine her in trousers, but she never cared what others thought, so she might have worn pants. She was a little thing."

"Small, but mighty, eh?" He clinked his mug against hers. "Kind of like you."

She laid her napkin on the table. "We ought to get home. Major and the chickens will be looking for something to eat soon."

"Changing the subject. All right, I'll bite." He raised his hand to get Kitty's attention for the check. Hopefully by autumn, he'd get her used to receiving compliments. Alternately independent and unsure, she was an enigma.

He paid the bill, and they were soon on their way. Fern knew the way home, so the traces lay loose in Jess's hands. The horse didn't need help finding the barn.

The miles passed in silence. What was she thinking about? Should he interrupt her reverie? She seemed content to watch the scenery without talking. Something else he admired about her. She didn't need to fill every moment with prattle like some women he'd met. Like his mother. He loved her dearly, but she could talk paint off a wall. Her sister was the same way, and when his aunt would visit, the drawing room echoed with their chatter.

Wheels rattling, the wagon rolled to a stop in front of the barn. Jess jumped down, then reached up to help Hannah to the ground. "I'll take care of putting everything away, but I've got a present for you to complete the celebration."

Her eyebrow shot up. "How could you know we'd hear from Mrs. Webb today?"

"I didn't. I've been planning this for a while, and now seems like the perfect time."

"But—"

"But, nothing. Close your eyes and wait here. No peeking."

She stared at him, uncertainty creasing her forehead.

He took her wrists and placed her hands over her eyes. "I won't be long." He trotted into the barn, then pulled the canvas cover off the rocking chair. Even in the dimness of the barn, the burnished cherry-colored stain gleamed. He carried the chair to the yard and plunked it on the ground in front of her. Would she like it? Heart pounding, he pulled her hands away from her eyes. "Okay, you can look."

Her gaze ricocheted from the rocker to his face. "You made this? For me?"

"Yes. Even as tiny as you are, the one inside seems to protest anytime you sit down. I thought you could use a stronger one."

She reached out, her fingers tentative as they stroked the curved headrest. "It's beautiful. I love it." She hurried to him and wrapped her arms around his neck. "I love it," she repeated. "And I'll treasure it always."

Jess's heart lifted. Perhaps he had a chance in winning over Hannah after all.

Chapter Twenty

Lightning flashed outside the cabin window. Moments later, thunder rumbled, shaking the tiny abode. Rain pummeled the roof and cut rivers into the yard between the house and barn. Jess added two more logs to the fire. The wood caught quickly, the flames dancing and pushing heat into the room. He rubbed his hands together, then held them close to the fire.

Behind him, Hannah washed the breakfast dishes. She hummed while she worked, her contralto voice low and smooth. He didn't recognize the tune, but she'd taken to singing hymns of late, so the song was probably a favorite from her past.

During the days since receiving the proof of ownership from Mrs. Webb, they'd settled into a routine of working the claim in the mornings and doing chores and repairs to the property in the afternoons. Evenings saw them playing checkers or whist. But today's gully washer had them inside for the duration. He'd recently finished shoring up the roof on the barn, so the animals should be warm and dry despite the storm.

He picked up his toolbox and went to the bedroom. Cocking his head, he studied the gap between the door and the frame. He lifted the latch, then swung the door back and forth. The bottom rail rubbed the floor, creating an arc-shaped scar, preventing the door from opening fully. His friend had many skills, but Quinn's woodworking left much to be desired. There didn't seem to be a square joint in the house.

With quick motions, he hammered out the hinge pins, then took off the door and set it aside. Using a pry bar, he removed the casings from around the frame, then grabbed his square and placed it against each corner to check the alignment. Not as bad as he'd originally thought. He could fix this with a few shims.

The hair on the back of his neck prickled, and he looked up. Hannah leaned against the counter, arms crossed.

"What?"

"You make the repairs look easy, and you obviously enjoy the work." She smiled. "I made do by learning how far I could open the door before the bottom would hit."

"Anyone can do this."

"Quinn couldn't. I can't." She tucked her hands into the pockets of her skirts. "My rocker is the prettiest piece of furniture I've ever seen. You're very good. Did you ever consider becoming a carpenter rather than a farmer?"

"For a fleeting moment, but then I came to my senses."

"I don't understand."

"Money. I didn't have it, and it takes cash to start a business, whereas my dad parceled off some of his land to me."

Her eyes gleamed. "After we split the proceeds from the mine, you'll have plenty to do whatever you want. Even a new career."

"I'm not going to take your money, Hannah." He rummaged in the box and dug out several thin pieces of wood, then wedged one into frame. "We talked about that, but I appreciate your offer."

"Are you always this stubborn?"

"Yes." He grinned. "Says the kettle to the pot."

She giggled. "Touché. But I'll be asking you again."

"I can use your help, if you've time to dawdle." He chuckled and pointed to the square lying on the floor. "Hold that against the corner while I insert the shims. Let me know when the corner lines up."

Her skirts swished as she bent to pick up the tool. The clean scent of her soap wafted past his nose, and he swallowed the desire to inhale. Deeply. Perhaps asking for her assistance was a mistake. Brow furrowed in concentration, she placed the square against the frame.

He shoved slim wedges into the frame one by one. He was nearly out of shims when she waved her hand. He climbed to his feet and looked over her shoulder at the tool. Her porcelain cheek was close. So close. A fraction of an inch away. He had a sudden urge to throw open the window to dispel the heat. Heat that wasn't emanating from the fireplace.

"Uh. Perfect. Now, we put the jambs back on, then hang the door." He took the square from her, and their fingers grazed. Prickles raced up his arm, and he tightened his grip on the tool to prevent himself from dropping it. Why did he have to turn into a clumsy oaf when she was so close?

She clapped her hands. "That tactic of shoving little pieces of wood around the door is brilliant. Did you think of that?"

"No, that's an age-old trick." But his chest swelled at her admiration. He could get used to the two of them puttering around her house together. He blinked and began to reframe the doorway, aware of her perusal. He nailed the last piece in place, then paused and gestured to her chair. "How about if you head over there and read?"

Her lips turned down. "I've got exactly six books, and I've read them all. Several times." She lifted one shoulder. "Maybe I'll do some mending."

"On your birthday?"

Her jaw dropped, and her mouth formed a perfect O. "How...?"

"Kitty. She figured you wouldn't say anything, so she told me. Apparently, she was right."

Face pink, she shook her head. "My birthday isn't anything special. I'm just another year older."

"Nonsense. Everybody deserves a celebration." He snapped his finger, pretending he'd just thought of an idea. Glad the subject of her birthday had come up sooner rather than later, he couldn't wait to present her gift. "I might have just the ticket. Don't move."

He grabbed his coat and hat, then turned, and wagged his fingers at her. "Stay right there."

"You're going out in this? Whatever you're going for can wait."

"No, it can't."

Hunching his shoulders, he splashed through the puddles and rivulets of water, then dashed into the barn. He hurried to the corner where he'd hidden the crate that arrived two days ago. He lifted the wooden box into his arms and made his way back to the house, the heavy burden slowing his progress.

He nudged open the door and clomped inside. He shucked his coat and hat and hung them on the hook. Water pooled on the floor.

"What is it?" She clasped her hands against her chest. Her face lit the room brighter than a dozen lanterns.

"Happy birthday." With his pry bar, he loosened the lid, then stepped back.

Tears filled her eyes as her joyful gaze shot from the box to him and back to the box. "You bought me a gift? Her voice broke as she lifted the lid and laid it at her feet. Her hands dug into the excelsior, then she pulled out a slim volume. "Books. You got me books."

Her dazzling smile sent his heart hammering. He'd buy her a wagonload of books if it meant she'd look at him like she was at this moment.

Chapter Twenty-One

A slim volume in her hand, Hannah lowered herself onto the couch. Jess set the crate on the floor in front of her. She rubbed the gilt lettering along the spine, and her lips moved as she silently read the title: *Mansfield Park*. How much had the collection cost him?

He perched on the arm of the sofa and pulled the book from her hands. His face shone as if on fire, and his eyes twinkled. "You have to look at all of them before deciding which one to read first."

"But—"

"You can ask me all the questions you want later. After you've checked out every book." His smile faltered. "You might have read a few of these. Some of the titles are fifteen or twenty years old."

"I will love whatever you've chosen." She pushed away more of the excelsior and lifted the volumes out one at a time. *Pride and Prejudice. Emma. Ivanhoe. Ode to a Nightingale. Frankenstein.* "I've heard this one is frightening."

"We can read that one together, and I'll keep the monsters at bay." He held up his fists. "As long as you don't make me read Keats."

She giggled. "We're in this together." She pulled out another book. "*Swiss Family Robinson.* I've always wanted to read this one. We'll do this one first."

"Keep going."

"There's more?"

"Yep." He looked like a cat who'd just discovered a jug full of milk.

Bending over the crate, she reached to the bottom. "*Rob Roy, The Pioneers, The Last of the Mohicans, Persuasion.* Oh, look! *'Twas the Night Before Christmas.*" She flipped through the pages. "There are illustrations." Her fingers hovered above the drawing. Tears sprang to her eyes. She'd never received a more special gift. "We'll save this one for December."

She slumped against the back of the sofa, the books piled on her lap. "Thank you, Jess. I will never forget what you've done, but you must return some of them. This many books cost a small fortune."

"Remember how you want to start a lending library?" He crossed his arms and looked smug. "This is my contribution, so you can't send them back."

"Any argument I come up with, you'll have a retort, won't you?"

He nudged her shoulder. "I've had lots of time to prepare for this."

Hannah pressed the book against her chest and sighed. "This is the best present I've ever received."

Jess cleared his throat. "Uh...you remember our...uh...tiff? In the barn with the paper? When you walked in on me, I'd just received the shipment notification. I couldn't come up with a plausible story, which is why I looked so guilty. I wish I was better at hiding things, so you didn't have to wonder if I was up to something terrible."

"Not being a good liar is an excellent trait to have." She rolled her eyes. "Trust me. And I'm sorry I was so awful about it. You'd been nothing but solicitous and kind, and yet I assumed the worst. Hardly fair of me." She narrowed her eyes. "How did you get the box here without my knowledge? We're always together."

"I made arrangements with one of the boys at the livery to deliver it while we were at the claim. It's been in the barn for two days."

She snapped her fingers. "Which is why you keep volunteering to collect the eggs and feed the chickens. And I just thought you were being nice." She raised one eyebrow. "I suppose it will be my job again starting tomorrow."

"Well..." His eyes crinkled at the corners as he grinned at her.

Pulse skipping, she swatted his arm and laughed. When had her heart felt this light? Not in many months, perhaps years. He'd come alongside her and eased her burden. Helping in big ways and small with never a complaint or judgment. He made her feel intelligent, clever, and beautiful. Traits she'd never assigned herself.

And she loved him.

Not for what he could do, but for who he was. A gentle man filled with integrity. One whose faith, though quiet, was strong and unwavering. A man who could help her be a better woman.

But there'd been no indication he reciprocated her feelings. Yes, he'd kissed her, but loneliness made people do crazy things. He was here to fulfill his vow to Quinn. Once he decided his commitment was complete, he'd be gone. Over the horizon and back to the life he had before receiving her husband's letter.

"A penny for your thoughts." Jess's voice broke through her ruminations.

Her face flamed, but she forced a saucy smile. "You'll have to pay more than that."

"I've—"

A knock sounded at the front door, and they exchanged a glance.

Jess rose. "Who would be out on a day like this?"

Hannah clutched the books tighter. "Someone bringing bad news."

"Or good." He opened the door.

Sheriff Fawley stood on the threshold, water streaming from his clothes. "I'm sorry to bother you folks, but I need to warn you that Asa Bennett is not taking too kindly to the news that you've proved your ownership to the claim. He spent time at the tavern getting drunk and telling people he's been wronged. He made it clear he plans to take matters into his own hands, saying he wasn't going to let some piece of paper get in the way of what's rightfully his."

A chill swept over Hannah, and she swallowed the nausea that roiled in her stomach. "Can't you arrest him for making threats?"

"We tried. He'd already left the bar by the time I heard what happened. I sent the boys to his place, but he wasn't there. We're still looking, but you need to be careful. Be extra vigilant."

"You think he's dangerous? Not just blowing off steam with the help of some liquor?" Jess's forehead creased.

"Yes. Drunk or sober, Bennett's a nasty piece of work."

Hannah's fingers trembled as she plucked at her skirts.

"All right. Thanks for coming out on a day like today. Can we offer you some coffee or time by the fire?"

"No. I need to get back to searching for this coyote." He touched the brim of his hat and dipped his head. "Good day, Hannah. Sorry to ruin your day."

"Can't be helped, Chet. Thanks for coming all this way in such terrible weather."

Jess grabbed his coat. "I'll be right back."

The men stepped outside, but the door failed to latch, so Hannah cupped her hand to one ear. With any luck she'd hear their conversation.

"You think you can protect our girl, Vogel?" The sheriff's voice was skeptical.

"Unfortunately, my time during the war honed my shooting skills, and I'm a fair hunter. Although I hate for it to come to that."

"Me too, but the man's been given any number of chances to handle this within the bounds of the law." He cleared his throat. "I'm deputizing you so that in the event...well...you know."

"Yep, I do."

Silence.

Then "Listen, Sheriff, thanks for trusting me with Hannah's protection. I know you care for her, but I need you to know I love her. I'm not going to let anything happen to her. Even if it means giving my own life to prevent her death."

Hannah gasped, then clapped her hand over her mouth. He didn't love her. He couldn't possibly. He said he knew Sheriff Fawley cared for her. Was Jess trying to get under the man's skin or prove something? But what? She gritted her teeth. Did she dare ask him? Did she want to hear his answer?

Chapter Twenty-Two

Dappled sunlight filtered through the trees as Jess followed Hannah on horseback. The day at the claim had been highly productive pushing away the memories of their frustrations when they'd worked for over a week with little success. With one eye on the pan and the other on the forest watching for Bennett, he'd been relieved when she decided to call it quits. He'd have been surprised if the man was foolish enough to try something when they were surrounded by dozens of people, but he couldn't take a chance.

The horses' hooves were muffled on the leaf-covered path, and birds flitted among the tree branches. His shoulders and back ached, but after weeks of hunching over the water, he'd built up enough stamina that his muscles no longer screamed at night. Hopefully, he wouldn't end up with a permanent hunch.

In front of him, Hannah slumped in the saddle. Her head bobbed in cadence with the pony's gait. Had she fallen asleep? He swallowed a grin.

She was tenacious at working the claim, and he'd end up on the sharp side of her tongue if he alluded to any weakness on her part.

His gaze slid back and forth, probing the woods for activity. Bennett didn't strike him as having the ability to sneak up on them, but Jess didn't want to underestimate the man. The hairs on the back of his neck prickled, and he shot a look behind him. Nothing. How long before the codger tried something?

Moments later, they entered the clearing, and the horses sidestepped. Major ground his teeth, and the pony swished his tail, evidence of their agitation. Hannah seemed to rouse as Jess stiffened. His hand went to his gun as he swiveled his neck surveying the area. What did the horses sense that he couldn't see?

"Hannah," he hissed. "Dismount and stick close to Fern. I'm going to check out the barn, then the house. I want you to stay out here until I'm finished."

Eyes wide and face ashen, she nodded. She slipped from the saddle and huddled close to the pony.

Jess clenched his jaw as he climbed to the ground. He hated to see her so frightened. When would this nightmare be over? He pulled his pistol from his holster and crept into the barn. He peered into stalls and behind hay bales. Kicking aside the pile of canvases, he tightened his grip on the weapon. Inside the coop, the chickens clucked, seemingly unconcerned.

"Jess!" Hannah's scream pierced the air.

Heart in his throat, he rushed from the barn.

She pointed toward the cabin with a shaking finger. A green cast colored her complexion, and she clapped one hand over her mouth.

His gaze followed her finger, and his stomach went taut. Someone...Bennett, no doubt...had left the remains of a mutilated fox in front of the door. Blood pooled beneath the carcass. No wonder the horses had spooked. The poor animal had obviously suffered, evidence of the man's unbalanced state of mind.

A gust of wind fluttered a paper nailed to the frame, and Jess strode forward. He snatched the parchment from the spike and perused the words scrawled across the page:

THIS COULD HAPPEN TO YOU. CLEAR OUT OR ELSE.

Whoever wrote this was savvy enough not to sign the threat, but no one other than Bennett had a beef with Hannah. How long before Sheriff Fawley and his men found the old coot?

"I'm going to check the house, but I doubt anyone is inside." He gestured to the remains. "He delivered his message."

She shuddered and wrapped her hands around her middle, her shoulders hunched. "What kind of person does this to a defenseless animal? The man is crazy."

"And very dangerous. That much is evident." Jess glanced at the cabin. " Wait here." He skirted the carcass and pushed open the door. Vacant. He marched across the room and nudged open the bedroom door.

Also vacant. He breath expelled in a loud rush, glad he wasn't forced into a showdown with the man.

He pivoted and hurried outside. "We need to notify the sheriff, but I need you to go inside and pack a bag. It's not safe here."

"But—"

"No argument. I'm not going to stay here like a sitting duck and neither are you. We'll find someone to handle the chickens." He frowned. "I'm going to join the posse looking for this guy, and I'd like you to stay with Kitty from the restaurant unless you have a better idea."

"No. I'm not looking to get killed either. No amount of money is worth that." Her eyebrows drew together as she snuck a peek at the fox. "What a waste of life. I'm not sure I can help you clean this up."

"We're going to leave it so the sheriff can see what we're up against. One of his boys will take care of it."

She pressed her lips together and gave the carcass a wide berth as she entered the house. He followed her, then leaned against the wall while she went into the bedroom to collect her clothes. She entered the living room carrying the valise, her posture stiff and guarded.

He grabbed the satchel, then walked to the couch. He picked up two of the books they'd oohed and aahed over just yesterday and slipped them into the bag. "The bright light in all of this is that you'll have some extra time to read."

Her giggle ended in a sob, and she caught her lower lip in her teeth.

Jess dropped the bag and enveloped her in his arms. His chin rested on her head as her arms snaked around his waist. Her body shook as she cried, and he rubbed circles on her back. "We'll get this guy. Right now, you're frightened and angry, but God is watching over us. Things are going to be all right." *Please, God.*

She nodded against his chest. "I'm sorry for falling apart." She sniffled and pulled away. "I don't mean to be such a crybaby."

With a tender finger, he raised her chin until she looked him in the eye. "You're one of the strongest women I know. This is a stressful and disturbing situation. I'd say a little crying is in order."

Eyes shimmering with unshed tears, she gave him a tremulous smile. "Thanks for being so understanding."

His heart banged in his chest as she gazed at him with a mixture of gratefulness and admiration, and a hint of fear clouding her eyes. A lock of hair had pulled loose from her braid, and he tucked the strand behind her ear before running his thumb down her jaw. Better get going before he did something stupid like kissing her. "I want to get into town before dark."

She blinked, then squared her shoulders and swiped at the moisture on her cheeks. "Of course."

He gave himself a mental slap for being so abrupt. "Hannah—"

"You're right. Daylight's burning." She rushed from the house.

Taking one last look around to ensure Bennett hadn't done anything inside, Jess stalked from the house. He mounted Major, then urged the horse forward. Slight pressure with his knees put the stallion into a canter, then a gallop as he followed Hannah toward town.

Thirty minutes later, they reached the edge of the settlement. Slowing the horses to a trot, they made their way down Main Street to the jail. Tying off the horses, they hurried inside.

Flushed and perspiring, Sheriff Fawley glowered.

Jess pulled off his hat. "We've had an incident."

The lawman's eyebrows rose to his hairline, and his lips thinned. "What? I've been in the saddle all day. We've had no luck finding Bennett, although we've seen lots of evidence of him."

"We've got more evidence. He left a *gift* at Hannah's cabin. The mangled corpse of a fox. It's obvious the poor animal suffered. A lot." He held out the letter. "And this was nailed to the house."

Sheriff Fawley perused the sheet, then tossed it on the desk, his face dark and thunderous. He pointed at Hannah. "This has escalated too far. You're staying in town. Pick a friend. I don't care which one."

"I've got my bag with me. I planned to ask Kitty to put me up."

"Finally, you show some sense. It's about time."

"How dare—"

Jess laid his hand on Hannah's arm. "Now's not the time. He's worried about you, and angry he hasn't been able to stop this guy."

"You're right I'm angry. He's crazier than a rabid raccoon, and I haven't managed to find him. I'm going to send two of the boys to her place, but I want you with me. We'll grab a few hours of shut-eye, then set out before dawn. There are some caves in the mountains I haven't check yet. With any luck, he's stupid enough to have a fire going, and we'll see the glow."

"Sounds good. I'll get her settled and be back in a bit."

"Do you have to talk about me like I'm not here?" She stood with her hands on her hips, head cocked. "I can hear you."

Even in her fear, she had gumption. He bowed. "My apologies. May I escort you to your lodging for the night?" He hoped she appreciated his attempts at levity. The next few days were going to be difficult.

Her frown dissipated as she gave him an exaggerated curtsy. She blew out a loud breath. "I'm sorry, Jess. Sheriff. You're just trying to keep me from harm. Let's go."

They headed outside and turned left. When they arrived at the restaurant, she laid her hand on his arm. "Listen, Jess, I wanted to let you know how much I appreciate all you're doing for me. Protecting me from a crazy person shouldn't be part of your promise to Quinn." She raised her eyes to his. "But I'm glad you're here. I don't know what I'd do without you, and I wouldn't want to be going through this with anyone else.

Chapter Twenty-Three

The ache in Hannah's shoulders bloomed into sharp pains that traveled to her lower back and hips. Standing on her feet for hours washing piles of dishes was more exhausting than a day at the river. And not remotely productive.

Two days had passed since Kitty had agreed to put her up, and her friend had talked her boss into letting Hannah help at the restaurant. But time was wasting. Every day that she wasn't at the claim ate at her. There was work to be done.

Kitty entered the kitchen with another pile of soiled plates and stacked them on the counter next to the sink. "Only a few more diners, then you can quit for the day. That was one of the largest crowds we've had in weeks." She blew an errant strand of hair out of her face, then retrieved a few coins from her apron pocket and laid them on the shelf above Hannah's head. "Your portion of the tips."

"People don't tip the dishwasher, and I don't need the money."

"We split the tips around here. I told you that yesterday. Buy yourself a new hat or give it to the poor. Makes no nevermind to me, but the money is yours."

"Fine." Hannah scrubbed at the dried food on one of the plates, her muscles protesting the movement. "This is my last shift. I really appreciate you letting me stay with you, but I need to go home."

"You can't." Kitty eyes widened. "The posse isn't back, which means that man is still out there. Probably waiting for you to lower your guard."

"If he was around, he would have been found by now." She swiped at the perspiration on her forehead with the back of her hand. "He's long gone, and it's perfectly safe for me to go home."

"Jess will kill me if anything happens to you." Kitty frowned. "I've got to get back to my customers, but we'll do something fun after work."

Hannah pressed her lips together as the waitress sashayed out the kitchen door and into the café. Kitty meant well, but enough was enough. Asa Bennett had left Dahlonega. Yes, he'd made that awful threat, but if he hadn't been found in forty-eight hours, he wasn't in the vicinity. He'd realized he was going to jail if caught, so he'd hightailed it out of town.

The first intelligent action the man had taken.

Wrinkling her nose, she rinsed the plate and started on another. Having something to do was better than moping around her friend's room at the boarding house, but not by much. Washing her own dishes was one thing, but cleaning up after strangers wasn't her idea of a good time.

An image of Jess's face pushed its way in her head, and she smiled. He'd have plenty to say about her being hunched over a kitchen sink, and the fact that she'd worn a dress two days in a row. She had to admit, she did like how feminine the outfit made her feel. Would he like the color? The deep-blue garment was one of her favorites, always improving her mood when she put it on.

Her pulse sped up. How long before he and the posse would either give up looking or return triumphant? Would Bennett surrender without a fight, or would the men have to resort to a gun battle. Goose bumps rose on her arms. *Lord, please keep them safe.*

Kitty clattered back into the kitchen with an armload of dishes. "These are the last of them." She squeezed Hannah's shoulder. "You're doing a great job."

"Thanks. I appreciate—"

"Don't start with that again. You're staying another night, and that's that." She fluttered around the kitchen putting away the clean plates and bowls. She grabbed a broom from the corner. "I'll sweep out front, then help you finish. We'll be out of here in a jiffy. Then we can go shopping." Her eyes lit up. "I've a hankering to make myself a new summer frock. Won't it be fun to pick out fabric?" Without waiting for an answer, she rushed from the room.

With a snicker, Hannah shook her head. The woman had more energy than a squirrel preparing for winter. If she wanted to look for dress material, Hannah would keep her company, but shopping was one of her least favorite tasks. Afterward, she'd pack her bag and head back to the cabin.

Thirty minutes later, the sink was empty and every piece of kitchenware put away. The counters shone, and the floor was spotless. Hannah sagged against the wall. She'd be glad to put this job behind her. She grabbed her wrap and went into the dining room.

Kitty stood at the open door talking to a tall, good-looking man. The waitress giggled and patted her hair.

Clearing her throat, Hannah walked toward them, slipping into her cloak. "I'm worn out, Kitty. I desperately need to put up my feet, if you don't mind. Perhaps we can shop together another day or your friend can accompany you."

Relief and guilt warred for supremacy on the young woman's face. "If you're sure."

"Absolutely."

"All right. I'll see you later."

Hannah dipped her head at her friend's visitor and left the café. The soles of her feet burned with every step, and she grimaced. Home. She needed to be in her own bed in her own cabin. She'd leave Kitty a note explaining everything. She increased her pace, then winced when her feet protested. Hobbling to the livery, she asked the stableboy to have Fern saddled in thirty minutes.

Her heart lightened, and she made her way to the boarding house. She was tempted to change into her jeans for the ride, but as backwater as

Dahlonega could be, most were scandalized by women in trousers. She stuffed her clothes and toiletries into her satchel, then took one last look around the room to ensure she hadn't forgotten anything. She snapped her fingers and went to the tiny desk in the corner. She pulled out a piece of parchment, some ink, and a quill. Hopefully, Kitty would understand her desire to get home.

Fifteen minutes later she was astride Fern and trotting down the street. The stableboy had been thrilled when she pressed her tip money into his hands. The sun warmed her back as she rode. She pressed her knees against the pony's sides to push her into a gallop. The wind pulled the pins from her hair, and it was soon streaming behind her as they rushed forward. The horse seemed just as excited as she was to put the town behind them.

She let out a whoop when the cabin came into view. Swinging down from the horse, she cringed when her tender feet hit the ground. She'd need to rein in her exuberance for a day or so. She led the pony into the barn, removed her saddle, and brushed her down. She gave her an extra rasher of oats, then fed the chickens who clucked and pecked the ground. "Stop complaining, girls. I'm sure Glenda and Bart took good care of you while I was gone."

Chores completed, she hurried into the house as fast as her tired body would let her. It was too early to climb into bed, but the couch was definitely calling out to her. With a sigh, she lowered herself on the cushions, propping her head on the pillow. She'd close her eyes for just a few minutes...

Hannah awoke with a start. Was that a noise? Was Jess home? She bolted upright, her grogginess gone. Or was Asa Bennett here? She strained to hear. Silence. Perhaps she'd only imagined the sound, or perhaps she'd been dreaming.

Wait. What was that smell? She sniffed deeply. Was that smoke?

Chapter Twenty-Four

Jess rotated his neck, then massaged his thighs. Two full days in the saddle had stiffened his muscles until they protested with each step his stallion took. The posse had followed several trails only to find a cold pile of ashes and trodden grass at the end of each one. Sheriff Fawley was the best tracker he'd ever seen, but Bennett remained elusive.

Nearly ten hours had passed since they'd found any evidence of the man's presence, and they'd just come up empty searching the small cave they'd found. The lawman's face was dark, his chin jutted forward, and his mouth set in a slash.

How much longer would they search before the sheriff admitted the trail was cold? Until Bennett was in custody, Hannah was in danger, but was the man still in the area? Did he know he was being hunted? If so, maybe he was smart enough to skedaddle.

With a deep sigh, Jess shifted, and the saddle creaked. No, the man was determined to get his hands on Hannah's claim and didn't seem inclined to leave. Who would have believed he was savvy enough to avoid capture for so long.

"Hold up, men." Sheriff Fawley raised his fist. "Gather round."

Horses snuffled, and hooves clopped as the posse drew into a circle. Jess patted Major's neck. Were they going to call it a night?

"Thank you for your hard work in searching for this varmint. Frankly, I thought we'd have caught him by now, but he's a sly one. There's been no clues to his whereabouts for hours, so either he's left the area, or we need to bring in a better tracker than me."

Conversation buzzed as the deputies and volunteers debated the question.

"Whatever the answer, you've been away from your homes long enough. We're gonna bed down for the night. Anyone who wants to leave is welcome to do so now or first thing in the morning. You should be able to make it back to Dahlonega in three or four hours."

Sheriff Fawley pierced Jess with a steely gaze. "I think you should head back. Probably should have left you with Hannah to start with, but I figured the more eyes we had searching the better."

A chill swept over Jess. Had the lawman seen something to indicate their prey had returned to town, or was he simply being cautious? "Agreed. I'll rest Major for a couple of hours, then be on my way."

"Sounds good. We'll set up camp here. There's good grazing for the horses, and the cave will provide shelter from the elements in case the temperatures drop tonight."

Jess dismounted with the rest of the men, and they tended to their horses. He murmured to the stallion as he uncinched the girth and removed the saddle. The stallion seemed to sigh with relief. "Yep, it's been a while since you and I spent so much time on the move. You've done well." He stroked the animal's neck. "But you're not done yet."

"Vogel." The sheriff strode toward him. "Since you're not familiar with the area, you won't have realized that we're circling Dahlonega. The man's not headed in one direction as if he was leaving. I think he realizes we're onto him, and he's playing with us. I want you to hole up in town with Hannah. You two will be safer than out at the cabin. It's too remote."

"Yeah, but if it comes to a shootout, innocent people could get hurt."

"True." The sheriff yanked off his hat, then shoved his fingers through his hair. "Do what you think is best to keep our girl safe."

"You can count on it."

Fawley gave him a long look. "You were serious when you said you loved her?"

"I'd never kid about something like that." Jess shoved his hands into his pockets. "I've only been here a couple of months, but I feel like I've known her all my life. She's the most intriguing, yet maddening woman I've ever met." He snorted a laugh. "And she's totally worked her way into my heart. I doubt she feels the same, but I'm hoping to win her over. She's smarter than I'll ever be, and I don't deserve her, but I hope she'll have me, nonetheless."

"You've got it bad. That's the most I've ever heard you say at one time." The lawman chuckled and clapped him on the shoulder. "But you're a good man. One filled with integrity and faith in God. Hannah doesn't need anything more than that. I'll be praying for you...both in keeping her safe and winning her heart."

"Thanks." The tightness in Jess's chest seeped away, and he rocked on his heels. "One step at a time."

"I've seen the way she looks at you. You're more than halfway home, friend." He wiggled his eyebrows, then patted Major's rump. "Godspeed, Jess."

Mind racing, Jess watched Fawley saunter toward the men. He spoke to a pair who were building the fire, and they guffawed, their teeth flashing in the dim light. Did the lawman know what he was talking about? Was Hannah developing feelings for him? Or was she merely grateful for the help and support he'd provided since Quinn's death?

He paced and prayed, his silent pleas to the Almighty Father determined and desperate. Noise from the camp lessened until only the occasional snore or muted rustle could be heard. Jess glanced at the moon. Time to go. He crept toward Major and patted the horse's muzzle before hefting the saddle onto the animal's back. With practiced motions, he tightened the girth, then slipped the bit between Major's teeth. Moments later, the tack was all in place, and he climbed into the saddle.

His thigh muscles ached, but the pain was worth getting back to Hannah. He leaned close to the horse's ear. "I hope you're in better shape than I am, old man."

Major bobbed his head as if in agreement, and Jess swallowed a chuckle. Moonlight guided them as they picked their way over rocks and uneven ground on the way out of camp. After they'd traveled for a few minutes, Jess nudged the horse into a trot. The stallion's long legs ate up the miles.

Two hours later, the landscape began to look familiar, and apparently the horse agreed because he picked up his pace. Jess gave Major his head, and the animal sped up to a full-fledged gallop. Thirty minutes later, the acrid smell of smoke wafted in the chilly night air. The odor was stronger than that of a chimney. Besides, who would be cooking in the middle of the night. Heart in his throat, he scanned the sky. An orange glow flickered above the trees.

"Hannah!" He slapped the reins, and Major surged forward with a loud whinny. They thundered down the well-worn path, Jess's breath ragged in his ears. *Please, God, not the cabin. It's everything she has.*

As he got closer to the property, dark smoke swirled and danced in the night air. He pulled his handkerchief over his nose and mouth, but his burning eyes teared as he strained to see. Major snorted in protest. He stroked the stallion's head. "I know it's awful, but hang tough."

He reached the clearing and gasped. Two-thirds of the cabin was engulfed in flames. Men and women had formed a bucket brigade from the river, but their efforts were in vain. God bless these people who'd come from far and wide to douse the fire. He dreaded telling Hannah about her loss.

Sliding from the saddle, he rushed to join the ranks, but movement to his left caught his attention. Someone bent over a huddled form wrapped in a quilt.

Hannah! His heart leapt to his throat, and he tore across the clearing. He knelt by her side, his stomach clenching at her appearance. Her eyes held a vacant gaze, and her shoulders were hunched forward. Smudges of soot marred her forehead and one cheek. Her bedraggled hair hung limp down her back. She never looked more vulnerable. Or beautiful.

"Hannah. Are you injured? Does anything hurt?"

She shook her head, and a single tear etched a trail through the dirt on her face.

He grasped her tiny hands in his. "Did you see anyone? Was it Bennett?"

"I don't know." Her voice was monotone. "I smelled smoke, and then I saw flames through the window. I ran outside, and the roof was on fire. I was so frightened, but then people started to come. They helped, but it's no use." Her lower lip trembled. "I've lost everything."

"What were you doing here?" He frowned. "You could have been killed."

"Don't yell at me. The posse had been gone for days. I figured Bennett was far away, and I was tired of being a burden on Kitty."

Before he could change his mind, he pulled her into his arms, and she melted into his embrace, laying her head on his shoulder. The cabin was gone, or would be soon, but she was safe—the only thing that mattered. He tamped down the panic that threatened to overwhelm him. If she'd died, his whole world would have been plunged into darkness.

Chapter Twenty-Five

The pungent odor of smoke tickled her nose as Hannah sifted through the few belongings that had been dragged out of the burned-out cabin, then transported to the church by some kind person after Jess convinced her to return to Kitty's. The only portion of the home that hadn't been affected was a small corner of the living room. The corner that held the rocking chair Jess had made and the crate of books. Had God left her these gifts, or was she seeing a miracle where there wasn't one?

After hours of fighting with the sheets and crying, she'd finally fallen into a restless sleep, then had been awakened as townspeople and miners alike had overwhelmed her with their generosity. One by one, they began to show up with armloads of clothing, shoes, kitchenware, and food; they offered to help her rebuild. What had she done to deserved their kindness?

Jess was conspicuously absent. After determining she was uninjured, he'd hitched Fern to the wagon and driven her back to town. On the way, he lectured her on returning to the cabin without protection. He hadn't called her a stupid woman outright, but his haranguing said that's what he thought. When she couldn't take any more, she'd hollered at him to stop the conveyance so she could get out and walk. Like Quinn, he'd made her feel like an incompetent, as if she was incapable of making wise decisions. That type of friendship she could do without.

He'd fumbled through an apology, then they'd ridden the rest of the way to Kitty's in an awkward silence. She'd mumbled a "Thanks for the ride" before scrambling out of the vehicle without a backward glance. The wagon sat outside the waitress's place for a long while before she finally heard it rattle away.

Hannah lifted one of the books from the crate and stroked the gold lettering on the spine. Her lower lip trembled, and she pressed her lips together. Since when was she such a crybaby? She clasped the volume close to her heart and shut her eyes. Last night's anger at Jess had been misplaced. He'd yelled at her, but his voice had been tinged with fear. He'd been afraid for her safety, but she'd let her temper get the best of her. Again.

"Forgive me, Lord. I have blessings galore, yet I continue to be hardheaded and ungrateful. Show me the way. I'm at a loss about what to do. Where to go. I've had enough of scraping the earth for gold." A tear rolled down her cheek. "And I feel so alone."

You have Me, My child.

Warmth like a quilt settled over her. "Yes, I do, Father." She cast her gaze toward the ceiling, and wry smile curved her lips. "Thank You for the reminder."

She sighed and sank onto a nearby chair. When he'd asked, she told Jess she'd start a library when she was finished panning. Why had she forgotten that dream? She didn't need him or any other man to help her begin the next chapter in her life. She glanced at the crate. Could she bear to use his gift as the foundation of the library? Did she want other people's hands on her special collection?

With a loud sigh, she put her head in her hands. Did she want to remain in Dahlonega, or were there too many memories? Good and bad. Sweet and bittersweet. She knew one thing for sure. Even if she stayed, she'd sell off the property and let someone else build their cabin in the woods. Her stomach hollowed. Would anyone buy the land? Bennett was still at large and might take out his schemes on the next owner.

The door opened, and Jess marched across the floor, a scowl etching deep lines on his face. "Were you going to leave without saying goodbye?"

"What?" She jumped out of the chair. "What are you talking about?"

"I went to Kitty's to see how you were faring after everything that happened, and she told me you were at the church packing."

"Of course, I'm packing. I can't exactly live here, and I need to sort the donations. People have been so benevolent, but there are items that don't fit or I'll never use, so I told the pastor I'd box those and set them aside for other needy folks. The rest I'll take with me once I decide what I'm going to do." She pierced him with a narrow gaze. "And where I'm going to do it."

"You're not leaving?"

Hannah crossed her arms. "What do you care? You spent most of the ride last night berating me."

"I'm sorry. I was out of line, but I was terrified at what could have happened."

"In other words, this is all about you and how you feel. How this situation impacted you."

"No!"

"Sure seems that way to me." She crossed her arms. "Look, I know you mean well, but I'm done. I've decided to sell off the claim or give it away. I don't care what happens to it. Anyway, your obligation is finished. You can now go back to whatever it was you were doing. Or try something new." Her throat thickened, and she swallowed the lump that formed. "Either way, I'm no longer your problem."

"I never felt like you were a problem." He stepped toward her, then hesitated. "I also came with news. Asa Bennett is dead."

"Dead?" She blinked as she tried to process the information. "How?"

Wohali came by first thing this morning to say that the one of the members of his tribe killed the man. After they heard about the fire, they tracked him down. Seems they don't take too kindly to people preying on innocent women."

"But we don't know for sure that he's the one that set it."

"Yes, we do. Apparently, he confessed to everything as he was dying, including killing Quinn and framing the Natives. Insisting to the end that he'd been wronged."

"That's sad."

"Yes, but his death means you're safe now. You can stay and rebuild. Keep working the claim as long as you'd like. You don't need to sell."

She shook her head. "But I want to. I meant what I said. I'm finished hunching over a pan of swirling water in the hope that a nugget or some flakes will materialize. I appreciate you coming by, and I'm sorry I lost my temper last night." She gave him a saucy grin. "You were trying to help me, even though your methods might have been a little suspect."

He chuckled. "You have no need to apologize. I deserved everything you said." He twisted his lips. "And everything you didn't."

Her face warmed, and she giggled. "I'm glad we're friends again." Her heart constricted. Too bad they'd never be more than that. She licked her lips and gestured to the crates. "I'm finished here, if you'd like to give me a hand at taking the items I'm keeping to Kitty's."

"I'd like that very much. But there's something I need to do first." Jess dropped to one knee and took her hands in his.

She gasped, and her pulse skittered. "What—"

"Shh. You've had your say." He stroked her hand. "I love you. In only three months, you have embedded yourself into my heart, my very soul. I can't imagine my life without you, and I hope you'll do me the honor of becoming my wife."

Tears sprang to her eyes. "I love you, too, and didn't dare to think you might feel the same way."

"I think I loved you from the first moment I saw you." He turned over her hands and kissed her palms.

Her toes curled as a warm sensation traveled to her shoulders, then shot down her spine.

Climbing to his feet, he cupped her face and gazed into her eyes. The air sizzled between them. "And I'm looking forward to a lifetime of showing you, but hopefully this is a start." He lowered his mouth to hers.

Her lips softened under his. What a start it was.

August, 1830

Epilogue

A carriage clattered down Main Street as Hannah pushed the perambulator onto the wooden sidewalk outside the lending library. She tucked the blanket around the tiny bodies of the twins, smiling when they cooed and waved their arms in unison. Most people would say the babies were too young at five months old to be out and about, but she wasn't most people.

She and Jess had been setting tongues to wagging for the last eighteen months. First, folks grumbled she'd married too soon after Quinn's death. As if a woman had much choice about being on her own. The same people were scandalized when Ursula Stanton had shown up in the spring unencumbered by a husband to purchase and operate a claim. At least once a day, Hannah heard someone accuse the woman of inappropriate behavior just for being single.

Her heart ached with a dull throb rather a sharp pain when she thought about Quinn these days. He hadn't been a perfect husband, but he'd loved her in his own way. She would have liked to have borne him a child, but God had other plans. Instead, she had not one but two beautiful children, a boy and a girl, who already seemed as stubborn as their parents.

Mrs. Rogers, one of the town's matriarchs tottered toward her. "Mrs. Vogel. I'm so glad I caught you." The ornate black silk bow on top of the woman's bonnet quivered. "You've got the babies. You are surely progressive, Mrs. Vogel, taking those children with you wherever you go."

"Yes, ma'am." Hannah swallowed a retort. "How may I help you?"

She waved a brown paper-wrapped volume. "That clever James Fenimore Cooper has a new book out, and I was able to procure a copy. All about a young woman who is abducted." Mrs. Rogers glanced behind her, then leaned close. "And there are pirates. Very exciting indeed. A perfect addition to your library." She pressed the book into Hannah's hands. "You'll want to get that on the shelves immediately. Now, I must be off. I left Mr. Rogers at the mercantile, and he can't be trusted to select the right items. Ta-ta."

Hannah gaped at the woman's retreating form. Initially, one of the most vocal opponents to the library, she was now one of its biggest supporters, often acting as if the idea to offer books free of charge was hers. Unaware of what changed the woman's mind, Hannah was grateful for her patronage, and her willingness to sway her friends into becoming allies as well.

She tucked the book, *The Water Witch*, if she remembered the title correctly, into the basket hanging from the buggy handle. Running the library was a mixed blessing. She had access to many of the latest publications, but limited time to read them. Perhaps she could convince Jess to curl up on the couch with her rather than working on the last dining room chair tonight.

After selling the claim, they'd purchased a two-story house at the edge of town. With six pillars and porches on both floors, the home was more grand than anything she ever thought she'd own. And own it, she did. Jess ensured both their names were on the deed. He'd kissed her soundly after carrying her across the threshold of the sprawling place with five bedrooms, and said he hoped they'd need to add more rooms to hold all the children. Her heart skipped a beat, and she shook her head. He always made her feel like a blushing schoolgirl.

Wheeling the baby carriage through the gate of the wrought-iron fence that surrounded their property, she turned her head toward the ever-present sound of the hammer. After filling their home with beautiful beds, tables, and chairs, he now crafted furniture for others in the barn behind the house. People came from all over Georgia to purchase his work, and she couldn't be more proud.

The babies chortled as she approached Jess who seemed unaware of her presence, intent on pounding a dowel into the top of a table leg. His muscles bunched under his cotton shirt, sweat stains darkening the fabric along his spine. She'd learned early on that he preferred to fit the pieces together with pegs than nails. Everything he made was a work of art. He'd denied her statement, but flushed and looked pleased the first time she'd said as much.

He glanced over his shoulder, and his face lit up, his eyes crinkling at the edges. He dropped the hammer and swept her into his arms. Lifting her off her feet, he swung her around until she squealed. He showered her cheeks and forehead with kisses, then set her down. "I missed you today."

"I missed you, too. But you know when I stay home, you play hooky." She wagged her finger at him. "And your customers wouldn't take too kindly to your being late with their orders."

"My wife, the taskmaster." He chuckled, then bent, and kissed the twins. "Did they behave?"

"As always, but I'm concerned they're getting spoiled by the ladies who come to the library."

"Nonsense. You can never show a child too much love."

"You're right." She wrapped her arm around his waist, and her fingers caught an envelope poking out from his back pocket. "What's this?"

He pulled out the letter. "I can't believe I forgot to tell you. Well, actually I can." He ran his finger along her jaw. "You fill my head when you're around, and I can think of nothing else."

"Enough sweet talk." She grinned and tried to snatch the envelope from his grasp.

Holding it out of reach, he pulled out the paper, then opened it with great ceremony. "Dear Mr. Vogel, I recently became aware of your beautiful furniture and have a need for a new dining room table and set of eight chairs. I would be most appreciative if you could fit me into your schedule to construct the aforementioned items of cherrywood at your earliest convenience. I leave the design up to you. I look forward to your favorable reply." Yours sincerely, John Q. Adams.

Hannah's eyes rounded. "Former President Adams?"

"Yes, ma'am." He waved the paper under her nose. "And there's more. He asked if you and the children would accompany me to make the delivery. He says he'd like to meet the...and I quote...'intriguing woman who single-handedly worked a gold claim.'"

"But I didn't," she sputtered.

"You can tell him all about it when you see him." He drew her into another embrace. "Unless, you don't want me to accept the order, Boss."

She snaked her arms around his neck and gave him a wicked smile. "Yes, but the president will have to wait his turn. You may start his project after you make the new cradle."

"Cradle? Cradle! Are you—"

"I have an appointment with the doctor tomorrow, but I do believe we're going to fill another one of those bedrooms."

He whooped, then pressed a tender hand against her stomach. "I'm sure Mr. Adams will understand."

Laying her hand over his, she sighed, happy tears filling her eyes. "Did you ever think we'd be corresponding with a man of such importance? God had been good to us."

"He has, but you and the children are my biggest blessings. Don't ever forget that."

"Never."

What did you think of *Gold Rush Bride: Hannah?*

Thank you so much for purchasing *Gold Rush Bride: Hannah.* You could have selected any number of books to read, but you chose this book.

I hope it added encouragement and exhortation to your life. If so, it would be nice if you could share this book with your family and friends by posting to Facebook (www.facebook.com) and/or Twitter (www.twitter.com).

If you enjoyed this book and found some benefit in reading it, I'd appreciate it if you could take some time to post a review on Amazon, Goodreads, BookBub, Kobo, Apple Books, or other book review site of your choice. Your feedback and support will help me to improve my writing craft for future projects and make this book even better. Thank you again for your purchase.

Blessings,
Linda Shenton Matchett

Want more romance set in the Old West? Read on for the first chapter of *Dinah's Dilemma.*

May 1870
Lincoln, Nebraska

Chapter One

Nathan Childs raced across the field toward his daughter as she toddled with determination toward the fire. How had he managed to let Florence get so far from his side? The three-year-old was fearless, and he knew better than to give her too much freedom. He'd already prevented her from crawling under the fence into the horse pen and trying to climb one of the massive sugar maples that sheltered the food tables at the town's Memorial Day celebration.

Perspiration trickled down his spine, and his shirt clung to his back as the midday sun beat down on his head and glared into his eyes. The morning had dawned unseasonably warm, and the temperatures continued to rise. Summers in Nebraska were known as scorchers, but May was early to be fighting heat and humidity.

"Florence," he shouted as he ran to gain the child's attention, but his voice was swallowed up in the myriad conversations, music, and laughter of Lincoln's citizens. Nebraska's capital had exploded in population over the last eighteen months, and Burlington and Missouri River Railroad's first train was due at the end of June. Sure to bring even more people. Not what he'd envisioned when he moved West after Georgianna's death.

Finally, close enough to grab her, he scooped Florence into his arms and pressed her close to his chest, her small body warm and soft. "What were you thinking, baby girl? Fire is bad. You need to be more careful and stay near me."

"No!" She arched her back and flailed her legs. "Fire is pretty, Daddy." Her face reddened, and she sobbed as if she'd lost her best friend. Tears dampened her cheeks, her blue eyes swimming.

His heart dropped. He hated when she cried. Her sobs made him feel as helpless as a newborn calf. He never knew what to do when she got like this. He hugged her closer and rubbed circles on her back in an effort to calm her.

"Sounds like someone's tired."

Nathan turned and nodded.

His best friend and the town sheriff, Alfred Denard, approached, a wide grin creasing his face below his black Stetson hat. "How about if you take a break and let Livvy watch her for a while. Looks like you both could use a change of scenery."

"Is it that obvious?"

Alfred chuckled as they headed for the cluster of women seated under the trees. "Sometimes I think you'd rather face the Mes Gang or Farrington Brothers than a crying little girl."

Nathan shrugged. "At least when I was chasing outlaws as a Pinkerton, I'd been trained and knew what to expect. Raising Florence is another whole ball of wax. Every day is different, so something I learned yesterday, doesn't necessarily work today." He blew out a deep breath as Florence quieted and tucked her thumb into her mouth. "I love her with my whole being, but maybe I should have let Georgianna's parents take her. I'm failing miserably."

"Do you think living with her grandparents is what's best for her?"

Nearing the blanket where Alfred's wife, Olivia, sat, Nathan paused and grimaced. "I don't know anymore. The thought of having to decide paralyzes me."

Livvy rose and held out her arms, her blonde hair swept into a tight bun at the base of her neck. She smiled, and her face glowed. "Are you going to let me spend time with your sweet little girl, Nathan? I've been aching to hold that child all day."

Florence chortled and reached for the buxom young woman. Nathan transferred his daughter into her waiting embrace, and his arms felt bereft. He shoved his hands into his pockets.

"Can I keep her through dinner, Nathan?" Livvy poked Florence's belly then rubbed noses with the giggling youngster. "We'll have lots of fun together, won't we?"

"You sure that's not too much time, Livvy?"

She shook her head. "Not enough, if you ask me." She jerked her head toward the corrals. "You boys head over to the pens and enjoy yourselves. The roping competitions should be starting soon."

Alfred ran his finger along her jaw then kissed her cheek, a starry-eyed look on his face. Married for three years, he still mooned over his wife, like a besotted schoolboy. Livvy had come from Atlanta as his friend's mail-order bride. Claiming love at first sight, they'd married immediately. "You holler if you need help, honey."

"I'll be fine." She winked at her husband. "Now, scoot."

Nathan pressed his lips together as his heart tugged. It had been too long since anyone looked at him like Livvy gazed at Alfred, but he had enough going on without saddling himself with a wife. He turned toward the festivities.

He couldn't ask for better friends than Alfred and Livvy. Two days after he'd arrived fifteen months ago, they'd shown up at his claim with food and friendship. Between the two of them, they'd arranged for some of the locals to transport his supplies from Omaha then pulled together a cadre of men to help build the house and barn. Livvy kept him fed when he didn't feel like eating in those early days of mourning after Georgianna's death. He'd figured moving to a new location would lessen the hollow feeling in his heart since she'd never lived in Nebraska, but his grief had followed him.

A city girl born and bred, she would have hated life on the plains, but he still missed her presence. Especially in the small things. Rustling up a stack of pancakes or sitting on the front porch watching the sun dip behind the trees, talking about everything and nothing.

The first year in Lincoln had been difficult, but rewarding. The crop had been decent, and he'd put aside some money for the future. Maybe to purchase the adjoining plot. Too soon to do so, but the idea was tempting. This year's wheat had done well and would be ready to harvest in another couple of months.

A stiff gust kicked up dust from the animal enclosures and swirled above the beasts. The acrid smell of manure clung to the breeze as it lifted his hat. Would he ever get used to the constant wind?

"All right, gents, time to see who's the best roper in the Lincoln." Barnard Johnson, a cattle rancher who owned the largest spread outside of town, stood in the center of one of the corrals, thumbs tucked in the waistband of his denim pants. A pair of ivory-handled pistols, Colts, if Nathan wasn't mistaken, hung from an ornate holster around his substantial belly. His boots gleamed.

Alfred jabbed Nathan with a sharp elbow. "You should take a turn. Show up the rest of the boys."

"No, thanks. I want to make friends not enemies."

"This is just a friendly competition."

"I'll pass, but you should take a turn. Confirm why you're the best sheriff in Nebraska."

"Because I can lasso the outlaws?" Alfred's chuckle rumbled in his chest. "Think I'll pass, too."

"Hey, Nathan. Aren't you going to show off those muscles of yours?"

Nathan cringed at the sound of Katrina Wainwright's strident voice that could send dogs and bats running for cover. She'd made her intentions clear at Christmas that he was the man for her despite his protestations to the contrary. Not one to be put off easily, she turned up at his side every chance she got. He squared his shoulders and pivoted on his heel.

Dipping his head in greeting, he forced a smile. "Good afternoon, Miss Wainwright. Are you enjoying today's event?"

Her giggle ended with a snort as she slapped his arm. "Katrina. How many times do I have to remind you to call me by my given name?"

"It wouldn't be proper, Miss Wainwright."

"We're not exactly in a Boston drawing room."

"True—"

"Hey, Katrina, watch this!" From inside the corral, one of Mr. Johnson's cowhands waved his hands over his head.

She turned, and Nathan took the opportunity to escape. Alfred followed close behind him. They strode to the six-foot tables piled with platters of food, grabbed a couple of plates, and chose several delicious-looking items. Nathan frowned. "That was a close one, but I feel bad for sneaking away."

"Don't. You've made it clear you're not interested. And after the incident with Florence when she took the child from the church nursery without your permission, she ought to know you'll never trust her." Alfred held an oatmeal cookie up to his nose and took a deep breath. "I do love my wife's baking." He took a bite and grinned. Shoving the rest of the treat into his mouth, he clapped Nathan on the back as he finished chewing. "I know how you can get rid of her."

Nathan narrowed his eyes. "I'm afraid to ask."

"Don't be. I have the perfect solution. You need a substitute girlfriend, and I know where you can get one."

"No. Before you say anything else, the answer is no. I'm not going to apply for a mail-order bride." Tears pricked the backs of his eyes. "You and Livvy are very happy, but I'm not in the market for a wife, and I don't think I'll ever be." He swallowed against the lump that had formed in his throat.

"I understand your grief. Don't forget I lost my first wife six years ago. But you can find love again. Unfortunately, the ratio of women to men out here isn't good, and your choices in Lincoln are limited." He wiggled his eyebrows. "Unless, you'd like to reconsider Miss Wainwright."

"Absolutely not." Nathan shuddered. "Despite her outward beauty, she's deceitful, and I could never love a woman like that. Florence and I are doing just fine with the two of us."

"Are you so sure about that? Your little girl needs a mother. You're not being fair to Florence. Please think about contacting Milly Crenshaw at the Westward Home and Hearts Matrimonial Agency." He squeezed Nathan's shoulder. "Now, as much as I enjoy time with you, I'm going to sit with my beautiful wife."

Nathan watched him leave, a jaunty air in his step as he threaded his way through the crowd to Livvy. She beamed as he approached then blushed after he bent and whispered something in her ear.

Was Alfred right? Could he find a woman he would love as he had Georgianna? He surveyed the townspeople, his gaze stopping to rest on Katrina. Full figured with a peaches-and-cream complexion, she had ebony-colored hair and deep-brown eyes. A gorgeous woman evidenced by the number of young men crowding around her like a flock of chicks.

But he couldn't get past her subterfuge. Plain and simple, she'd lied then claimed the whole thing was a misunderstanding. Should he try to find an honest woman who would love Florence as her own? Did this Milly Crenshaw have the answer? Surely, anyone she sent couldn't be any worse than Katrina.

Acknowledgments

Although writing a book is a solitary task, it is not a solitary journey. There have been many who have helped and encouraged me along the way.

My parents, Richard and Jean Shenton, who presented me with my first writing tablet and encouraged me to capture my imagination with words. Thanks, Mom and Dad!

Scribes212 – my ACFW online critique group: Valerie Goree, Marcia Lahti, and the late Loretta Boyett (passed on to Glory, but never forgotten). Without your input, my writing would not be nearly as effective.

Eva Marie Everson – my mentor/instructor with Christian Writers' Guild. You took a timid, untrained student and turned her into a writer. Many thanks!

SincNE, and the folks who coordinate the Crimebake Writing Conference. I have attended many writing conferences, but without a doubt, Crimebake is one of the best. The workshops, seminars, panels, critiques, and every tiny aspect are well-executed, professional, and educational.

Special thanks to Hank Phillippi Ryan, Halle Ephron, and Roberta Isleib for your encouragement and spot-on critiques of my work.

Thanks to my Book Brigade who provide information, encouragement, and support.

Paula Proofreader (https://paulaproofreader.wixsite.com/home): I'm so glad I found you! My work is cleaner because of your eagle eye. Any mistakes are completely mine.

A heartfelt thank you to my brothers, Jack Shenton and Douglas Shenton, and my sister, Susan Shenton Greger for being enthusiastic cheerleaders during my writing journey. Your support means more than you'll know.

My husband, Wes, deserves special kudos for understanding my need to write. Thank you for creating my writing room – it's perfect, and I'm thankful for it every day. Thank you for your willingness to accept a house that's a bit cluttered, laundry that's not always done, and meals on the go. I love you.

And finally, to God be the glory. I thank Him for giving me the gift of writing and the inspiration to tell stories that shine the light on His goodness and mercy.

Other Titles
Romance

Love's Harvest, Wartime Brides, Book 1

Love's Rescue, Wartime Brides, Book 2

Love's Belief, Wartime Brides, Book 3

Love's Allegiance, Wartime Brides, Book 4

Love Found in Sherwood Forest

A Love Not Forgotten

On the Rails

A Doctor in the House

Spies & Sweethearts, Sisters in Service, Book 1

The Mechanic & the MD, Sisters in Service, Book 2

The Widow & the War Correspondent, Sisters in Service, Book 3

Love at First Flight

Multi-author Series

A Bride for Seamus (Proxy Brides, 48)

Dinah's Dilemma (Westward Home and Hearts Mail-Order Brides, 10)

Rayne's Redemption (Westward Home and Hearts Mail-Order Brides, 15)

Legacy of Love (Keepers of the Light, 10)

Vanessa's Replacement Valentine, (Brides of Pelican Rapids, 13)

Mystery
Under Fire, Ruth Brown Mystery Series, Book 1

Under Ground, Ruth Brown Mystery Series, Book 2

Gold Rush Bride Hannah

Under Cover, Ruth Brown Mystery Series, Book 3
Murder of Convenience, Women of Courage, Book 1
Murder at Madison Square Garden, Women of Courage, Book 2

Non-Fiction
WWII Word Find, Volume 1

Biography

Linda Shenton Matchett writes about ordinary people who did extraordinary things in days gone by. She is a volunteer docent and archivist at the Wright Museum of WWII. Born in Baltimore, Maryland, a stone's throw from Fort McHenry, she has lived in historical places most of her life. Now located in central New Hampshire, Linda's favorite activities include exploring historical sites and immersing herself in the imaginary worlds created by other authors.

Website/blog: http://www.LindaShentonMatchett.com
Newsletter signup (receive a free short story): https://mailchi.mp/74bb7b34c9c2/lindashentonmatchettnewsletter
Facebook: http://www.facebook.com/LindaShentonMatchettAuthor
Pinterest: http://www.pinterest.com/lindasmatchett
Amazon: https://www.amazon.com/Linda-Shenton-Matchett/e/B01DNB54S0
Goodreads: http://www.goodreads.com/author_linda_matchett
Bookbub: http://www.bookbub.com/authors/linda-shenton-matchett